The
Matchmakers

The Matchmakers

Janet Dailey

OPEN ROAD

INTEGRATED MEDIA

NEW YORK

ISBN 978-1-4976-3959-1

This edition published in 2014 by Open Road Integrated Media, Inc.
345 Hudson Street
New York, NY 10014
www.openroadmedia.com

The
Matchmakers

Introduction

Introducing Janet Dailey's AMERICANA. Every novel in this collection is your passport to a romantic tour of the United States through time-honored favorites by America's First Lady of romance fiction. Each of the fifty novels is set in a different state, researched by Janet and her husband, Bill. For the Daileys it was an odyssey of discovery. For you, it's the journey of a lifetime.

Preface

When I first started writing back in the Seventies, my husband Bill and I were retired and traveling all over the States with our home—a 34' travel trailer—in tow. That's when Bill came up with the great idea of my writing a romance novel set in each one of our fifty states. It was an idea I ultimately accomplished before switching to mainstream fiction and hitting all the international bestseller lists.

As we were preparing to reissue these early titles, I initially planned to update them all—modernize them, so to speak, and bring them into the new high-tech age. Then I realized I couldn't do that successfully any more than I could take a dress from the Seventies and redesign it into one that would look as if it were made yesterday. That's when I saw that the true charm of these novels is their look back on another time and another age. Over the years, they have become historical novels, however recent the history. When you read them yourself, I know you will feel the same.

So, enjoy, and happy reading to all!

1

Y"our supervisors at the hospital recommend you very highly, Miss Darrow." The blond-haired woman glanced up from the papers in her hand and smiled politely at the young woman seated in front of her desk. "What prompted you to quit?"

"Actually it was a combination of reasons." Kathleen Darrow folded her hands primly in her lap, silently wishing she didn't feel so defensive. "I had four years of nurse's training and three more years working as a nurse. So for the last seven years my life has revolved around the hospital. There's more to the world than that, and I'd like to see what there is."

"In the form you filled out for the agency, you mentioned the night work as a reason. I imagine that particular shift would interfere a great deal with your social life."

Kathleen guessed that the woman interviewing her was barely two years older than herself. The name plaque on her desk identified her as Lorna Scott. She was very attractive and smartly dressed in a dusty rose pantsuit that complemented the tawny blond of her hair. Her aura of sophistication and poise made Kathleen feel gauche and uncertain. It was a ridiculous sensation when she knew how well her olive green suit showed off her slender figure, match-

1

ing the green flecks in her hazel eyes and accenting the fiery auburn high-lights in her brown hair.

"First, Miss Scott," Kathleen replied with a self-deprecating smile, "you have to have a social life before your work can interfere with it."

Laughter flowed easily and musically from the blonde. "You are destroying my illusions about nurses! I always picture them fighting off a patient with one hand while fending off the advances of a young intern with the other."

"There are some patients who think a massage means something else," Kathleen admitted, "but very few in my experience. And as for interns, ask me about bedpans and I could probably tell you more," she added with dry humor.

To deny that she had a social life wasn't exactly true. There was always Barry. The problem was Kathleen regarded him as more of a distant cousin than a boyfriend. He was Mr. Reliable, always there to pick up the pieces when a romance ended. Lately there hadn't been any pieces to pick up, so Barry provided her company and a ready escort.

"What type of position would interest you? Obviously you want to stay away from a hospital environment." Lorna Scott smiled with understanding and amusement.

"I honestly don't know what kind of work I would like," Kathleen admitted, shaking her head in faint bewilderment. "My experience has been strictly in nursing, yet I would like to get away from the medical profession for a while. I don't know what other type of position I'm qualified to hold."

"Let me see what openings our agency has available," Lorna Scott suggested, reaching for a card file on her desk. "I'm sure we'll find something."

I hope so, Kathleen thought silently as the woman began flipping through the index. Her friends, nearly all fellow nurses, had thought she was crazy to hand in her resignation without having another job lined up, but Kathleen had chosen not to listen to their well-meaning advice. There was enough money in her savings account to keep her going for a few months and she had known that if she didn't make a complete break from the hospital while she was determined to do so, she would never do it.

As for her future employment, she was open to any suggestion. She would willingly clerk in a department store or serve tables in a restaurant if need be. She knew she could always return to nursing.

It wasn't as though she didn't enjoy her work or find it rewarding. Her life had simply fallen into a rut and she wanted to blaze a new trail. With luck this employment agency would offer her a new horizon. Anything was better than her view of the old one.

"Have you had any experience with adolescents?" The other woman's question broke in on Kathleen's train of thought.

"I've worked in the pediatrics ward." A smile tugged at her mouth, bringing a pair of dimples into play. "And I'm the oldest of seven children, so I suppose that gives me some experience."

An agreeing smile touched Lorna Scott's face as she extracted the card from a file. "We have a client who's looking for someone to take care of his two children. Let's see." She consulted the writing on the card. "They're both girls. One is twelve and the other is ten."

"It sounds as if it's more supervision than actually taking care of them," Kathleen commented, her interest mounting as she contemplated the position.

"Our client is away from home a great deal and the job would require that you live in. It would also entail some housekeeping and cooking." Lorna Scott tipped her head to the side in resignation. "I can't say that it's a position that would help your social life."

"No, that's true." Yet it did have some compensations. While she wouldn't actually have a great deal of free time, there would be a considerable amount that she could spend as she wished. Two nearly teenaged girls would not require her constant attention or need to be entertained.

Her mother had always declared that Kathleen was a homemaker at heart. She certainly enjoyed working around her small apartment, cooking and cleaning and redecorating when the budget allowed. She had always looked forward to the day when she would have a home of her own. Of course, her dream had always included a husband. And there wasn't any applicant for that position on the horizon, unless one counted Barry, which Kathleen didn't.

"Still," Kathleen added after several seconds of consideration, "the job does sound interesting."

"Your experience and background would meet the requirements." The salary offered, in addition to meals and lodging, was generous. "You will have one day off a week and one weekend a month. The girls will stay with a relative during those times. Once the summer vacation is over and they're back in school, you would have more free daytime hours to yourself."

The more Kathleen thought about it, the more appealing the job sounded. Summer days with two girls would invariably mean a lot of time spent at the beach, swimming and lazing in the sun. It wouldn't be much different from playing around with her younger sisters and being paid for it. It was certainly worth looking into further.

As Kathleen started to say she was definitely interested in the job, her interviewer spoke. "About the only problem you might run into is that Mr. Long did request that the woman be older, more mature. A mother image, I suppose, as opposed to a sister. Unfortunately we haven't been able to find a qualified woman who is able to leave her own home to live in, so perhaps he'll concede that requirement. If you're interested, I can telephone for an appointment."

"I *am* interested," Kathleen stated definitely.

"Excuse me a minute while I see what I can arrange." Lorna Scott rose from her desk, taking the index card with her as she left the small room.

Kathleen waited silently, concealing her impatience. As a nurse, she had learned to control her emotions, whether anger, joy or sorrow. The first was not always easy, since the glint of red hair indicated a temper as quick to flare as a match.

It had surfaced often as a child, but with six other children, her parents had not had the time nor the patience to allow her to indulge in tantrums. Generally Kathleen counted to ten, waited until she was alone, then vented her wrath on some inanimate object. For the most part it had provided a successful method for releasing her frustrations.

"Good news," said Miss Scott, stepping back into the office. "I've arranged an interview for you this Saturday at one-thirty."

Kathleen leaned forward eagerly, wanting to wipe away the obstacle in her path. "What did he say when you mentioned my age?"

"Mr. Long is out of the country. I talked to Mrs. Long, his aunt, whom you will be seeing. I didn't have an opportunity to say more than that you were younger than he had requested. But it seems that there've been so few applicants for the position that Mrs. Long is willing to see anyone. She's staying with the girls until someone can be hired. Her only comment was that she was too old to keep up with two active girls." Lorna Scott smiled reassuringly. "I think that bodes very well for your chances."

"It might." Mentally Kathleen had crossed her fingers, discovering that she really wanted the job, providing that everything was as it seemed on the surface.

A slip of paper was handed to her. "Here are the directions to Mr. Long's home. It's out in the country near the coast of Delaware Bay. It shouldn't be difficult to find."

Glancing at the written directions, Kathleen nodded agreement. "I'm familiar with the coast roads. I think I know exactly where this is."

"In the meantime, I'll check through the rest of our openings to see if I can't find something else you might be interested in, just in case this one doesn't work out. I'll phone you at your apartment if I find anything," the other woman promised.

"I'm usually always there during the day." Kathleen slipped the directions into her bag.

That evening she was seated at a large oval table with three of the nurses from her old hospital and the ever-constant Barry. The remnants of a pizza were in the middle.

"Oh, Kathleen!" The last syllable of her name was released in hooting laughter by Maggie Elliot. "You aren't seriously interested in the job? You'd be

4

nothing but a glorified nanny and housekeeper. Surely you want something more exciting than that!"

"It isn't excitement so much that I want as it is a complete change of scene. I want to get away from regimentation and set hours and schedules," Kathleen tried to explain.

"Yes," Maggie sighed mockingly. "She probably wants to carry on intelligent conversation with the normal people. Imagine never having to explain again, 'The operation is over, Mrs. Jones. You're in the recovery room now and you're going to be just fine.' I sometimes think they should have a recording of that to play over and over again."

Darla, the more serious of the trio, spoke up. "Do you really think you'd like a job like that, Kathleen?"

"Why not?" she shrugged in answer.

"If those two girls are anything like my sister," Betty inserted, "I can give you a sound reason. They're probably know-it-all little brats who've been spoiled rotten."

"It's possible," Kathleen conceded. The same thought had occurred to her, but she was prepared to keep an open mind.

"Did you ask what happened to the last nanny?" teased Maggie.

"No," Kathleen admitted with a good-natured smile. "The only thing I know is that Mr. Long's aunt is taking care of them now. She evidently feels she's too old to make it a permanent arrangement."

"I bet I'm right then." There was a knowing nod from Betty. "If their aunt can't control them, they must really be holy terrors."

"What about their mother?" Darla asked. "Is she dead or is she divorced from this Mr. Long?"

"I really don't know. I didn't ask," Kathleen answered.

"What about Mr. Long?" Maggie tipped her head of curling blond hair on one side, a curiously bright light in her blue eyes. "What does he do for a living, Kathleen?"

"I don't know." She was beginning to sound like a broken record. "The woman at the employment agency said that he traveled a great deal and that he was out of the country now, but she didn't indicate the type of business he was in."

"Weren't you curious?" Maggie grinned in frowning amazement.

"Not really, I—"

"Maybe he's tall, dark and handsome," Betty interrupted. "Imagine living in the same house with someone like that!" She rolled her eyes suggestively.

"Or maybe he's short, fat and bald," Kathleen laughed. "Honestly, you girls are hopeless. I haven't even been interviewed yet. I don't even know for certain if I'll take the job if it's offered to me."

5

"I think you're crazy if you do." Maggie took a quick sip of her Coke. "It's one thing to be tied down to a home and children when you're married and another to do it voluntarily in someone else's home and with someone else's children. Think of the responsibility involved!"

"It wouldn't be any more responsibility than the health and welfare of a patient in the hospital." Kathleen airily waved aside that argument.

"It might not be so bad if you were to be living in town," Betty murmured sympathetically, "but out in the country, there just won't be anything for you to do."

"I love the country," Kathleen protested. "You're all forgetting that I was born and raised outside the city limits of Dover. It won't be anything new for me."

"You haven't said a word, Barry," Maggie commented. "What do you think about it?"

Barry ran his fingers through the side of his sandy brown hair, a stalling gesture to gain the time to consider his answer. In all the years Kathleen had known him, he rarely said exactly what was on his mind.

"Kathleen is certainly old enough to know what she wants. If she thinks this job is what she wants, I hope she gets it," he answered slowly.

"Yes, but with her free time so limited, you'll hardly ever be able to see her. It will be worse than when she worked the night shift," Betty pointed out. "Truthfully, Barry, is that what you want?"

"I don't know why I won't be able to see her as frequently as I do now," he said, clearing his throat nervously, "unless there's some restriction about her having visitors."

"That's one of the things I'll have to find out, if I'm offered the job and if I decide to take it," Kathleen inserted, emphasizing the fact that they were all discussing something that might not happen.

"Well, you're going to have to find a job sooner or later," Darla remarked. "Your savings account isn't going to last forever."

"Do you know what I've always thought I might like to try?" Maggie studied the ice in her glass with quiet contemplation. "I was always going to apply for a job as a nurse on a cruise ship. Why don't you do that, Kathleen?"

"It would be a waste of time. I get seasick," she laughed.

"If you can't find a job, you know you can always come back to the hospital," Darla reminded her.

"All that training, Kathleen," Betty sighed. "It's an absolute shame to let it all go to waste."

"Nothing is a waste. And who knows?" Kathleen lifted her hands palm upward. "I might not like it on the 'outside' and go back to being a nurse."

"Or you might get married," Maggie twinkled, casting a sideways glance at Barry.

6

Darla intervened with the suggestion that Kathleen might want to go back to the university and obtain a teaching certificate. The subject was gratefully diverted from Maggie's innuendo of marriage between Kathleen and Barry.

Kathleen believed she had heard the last of it until she and Barry were sitting at the small breakfast table in her apartment having coffee. The other three had gone to a movie that was in its first-week run.

Barry ran his fingers through his hair and slid a tentative glance from his coffee cup to her. "Kathleen, would you—like to get married?"

A frozen stillness held her motionless for an instant. His careful wording brought a silent sigh of relief. At least he had suggested marriage and not actually proposed.

"No, I don't think so, not right now anyway. Besides—" she smiled crookedly "—why should we spoil a beautiful friendship?"

It was a half-truth. She wanted to get married, but not to Barry. The problem was Mr. Right hadn't come along. In her heart, Kathleen believed that Barry knew this, although she had never explained it in so many words.

It was a shame really that she wasn't in love with him. Barry was a nice, sensitive and fairly attractive man. He would make an affectionate husband and a loving father. But for someone else, not her. Nothing happened when she was with him, not even a warm glow. When she married, it would be for love and no other reason.

When Barry left a half an hour later, satisfied with a light kiss at her apartment door, Kathleen couldn't believe that he was in love with her either. They had become a habit with each other, a habit they were both reluctant to break since it kept the loneliness at bay.

No doubt Maggie's comment about marriage had thrown Barry off balance. He had considered Kathleen's actions in quitting her job at the hospital as impractical and illogical. He hadn't really understood her restless need to seek a different horizon. Neither did she completely. The hesitant offer of marriage had probably been made because Barry thought that might be what she wanted.

Kathleen sighed. Not working left her with a lot of time to think. In some respects that was good, but she certainly would be glad when she found a job. There had never been any time for idleness in her life, not in childhood when being the oldest of seven meant she had to help her mother to keep house and care for the younger children, and not as a nurse.

Maybe she would be lucky with her interview on Saturday.

The Long house was easy to find, as she suspected it would be. A mile from Delaware Bay, it was an old white clapboard house two stories tall with black shutters at the windows. There was a quiet elegance about it, with its well-kept lawns and large shade trees.

The atmosphere around it was distinctly friendly and hospitable. Kathleen had the strange sensation of coming home as she halted her small Volkswagen in the driveway. Remembering Betty's warning that the two girls were probably spoiled brats, she smiled. It was impossible to believe it when she gazed at the home they lived in.

Curiosity moved her to the front door. She wanted to see the inside and find out if it lived up to the expectations of the outside. It was barely past one o'clock when she rang the bell. Her hazel eyes had a dominant sparkle of green flecks, her attractive features animated by the excitement of anticipation.

The door was opened by a slender girl, a few inches shorter than Kathleen. Her tawny blond hair was cut in a short boy's style to frame her face and its tip-tilted nose. Smoke-gray eyes ran over Kathleen in cool appraisal.

This had to be one of the girls, obviously the older, Kathleen decided. There was nothing churlish or insolent about her expression, only a considering kind of curiosity. For the first time Kathleen wondered what the two girls' reactions would be to a stranger being hired to look after them.

"Hello, I'm Kathleen Darrow," she introduced herself, a dimpling smile of friendliness curving her mouth. "I have an appointment for an interview at one-thirty."

"We've been expecting you," the girl nodded, an enigmatic light suddenly entering her gray eyes. "Come in, please." The door was swung open wider to admit Kathleen. "I'm Annette Long. Would you come this way?"

Kathleen stepped into the small entry hall and glimpsed the wainscoting of walnut paneling on the walls before she was ushered through a doorway on her left.

It was a study, casual and comfortable with plush shag carpeting of olive green. A fireplace was on an outer wall, made out of gray brick laced together with black mortar. Diagonally facing the fireplace was a small sofa in a tartan of olive green and black against an ivory-gray background.

The slender blond-haired girl walked to the walnut desk that almost filled the narrow side of the room. Kathleen's attention shifted with her, noting the pair of chairs covered in ivory leather. One was occupied by a younger girl with medium-length dark hair and a faint dimple in her chin. Her eyes were blue and she gazed apprehensively at Kathleen.

"This is my sister Marsha," Annette Long announced, settling into the black swivel rocker behind the desk and resting her forearms on its top. "Marsha, this is Kathleen Darrow. She's come about the job."

8

Something in the inflection of her voice seemed to put more meaning in the casual announcement. Or was it the tension Kathleen detected in the younger girl? Marsha did not possess the same air of confidence as her older sister.

Their coloring, the contrast between blond and brown hair, and gray and blue eyes, seemed to deny they were sisters. Yet their delicate facial structures were very similar. Kathleen wondered briefly which girl took after which parent.

"Hello, Marsha," she said. "You must be the youngest."

"I'm eleven. Annette is twelve." Marsha nibbled slightly at a corner of her lip and tried to smile.

"Actually Marsha is ten and a half," Annette corrected, then with a wave of her hand she indicated the empty chair in front of the desk. "Have a seat, Miss Darrow."

Kathleen took the chair and set her bag on the floor beside her. "Thank you. You have a very lovely home." She glanced around the room again, silently wondering where the girls' aunt, Mrs. Long, was.

"We like it," Annette shrugged. "How old are you, if you don't mind me asking?"

"Twenty-five." As Kathleen answered, she noticed Marsha's gaze skitter questioningly to her sister, who merely smiled and nodded as if the reply was satisfactory.

"And you were a nurse before you applied for this position, is that right?" Annette continued.

"Yes, that's correct. I've been a fully registered nurse for the last three years," Kathleen replied.

"What made you give up nursing?" The blond girl leaned back in the swivel rocker, clasping her hands in front of her, totally composed.

Kathleen hesitated, covering up her confused frown with a smile. "Excuse me, it's not that I object to answering your questions, but I'm supposed to be interviewed by your aunt, Mrs. Long. I'm sure she'll ask the same questions you have. Perhaps we should wait until she joins us."

"Actually Helen is our great-aunt," Annette corrected, not the least put off by Kathleen's suggestion. "She married our grandfather's brother. He died ages ago." She pushed herself out of the swivel chair and walked around to the front of the desk, leaning against it to study Kathleen with a solemnly straight face. "Helen won't be joining us immediately. You see, we—that is, Marsha and myself—am screening applicants for her."

"I see." Kathleen wasn't exactly certain if she did see. It was a novel experience to realize she was about to be interviewed by a twelve-year-old girl.

"It's very logical and practical, actually. After all," Annette continued, "whoever is hired to look after us is going to be living with us day after day. Naturally we want to be certain that whoever gets the job is going to be compatible with us. It will make things much easier all the way around, don't you agree, Miss Darrow?"

Kathleen wanted to laugh, amazed and amused by the turn of events, but she couldn't do that when both girls were so completely serious. Besides, there was a great deal of truth in the idea.

"Yes, I do agree," she admitted, feeling the indentations deepening in her cheeks as she tried to conceal her amusement.

"I'm glad." Annette smiled, with a youthfully charming grin. "That puts us off to a good start right away. Tell me, what are your hobbies?"

"I enjoy swimming, playing tennis, reading, cycling, listening to music and sewing. Not necessarily in that order of preference."

"What kind of music do you like?" Marsha spoke up. "Popular music?"

"Basically I like all kinds of music, including the popular beat tunes," Kathleen agreed.

"Did you leave nursing because of a man?" Round gray eyes watched Kathleen's startled expression with unblinking innocence.

The frankness of the question halted Kathleen for a split second. "No, it wasn't a man or any broken love affair," she answered, remembering how romantically fanciful her own younger sisters had been at that age, and probably herself, too. "I simply decided that I wanted to see something more of the world than the walls of a hospital."

"You're young and attractive." Again Annette ran an appraising eye over her. "Surely you have boyfriends."

"Well—" Kathleen hesitated. She supposed Barry would count as a boyfriend. "Yes, there is a man I've been dating recently."

"Are you going to marry him?" The abrupt question was immediately followed by an explanation. "You see, Miss Darrow, if you're in love with the man and are planning to marry him any time soon, then it's really pointless to consider you for the position. A few months from now we might have to go through this same rigmarole again."

"We're good friends, that's all. I'm not contemplating marriage with anyone at the present time." Kathleen again checked the smile that persistently teased the corners of her mouth.

"Don't you want to get married?" Marsha looked momentarily worried as her dark eyebrows puckered together in a slight frown.

"Yes, some day, when I meet the right man."

"Naturally, that's what all we girls want," Annette declared in a pseudo-adult voice, sending a quelling look at her sister. "Do you have any brothers or sisters?"

"Six of them," Kathleen admitted, curiously glancing from one to the other. "Four sisters and two brothers. I'm the oldest."

"Does your family live near here?"

"About sixty miles away. I usually try to see them once a month."

"Would it bother you, living out here in the country? I mean, with just us two when father is away?" Annette questioned.

"Aunt Helen is terrified someone will break into the house," Marsha explained hastily. "Every night she runs around locking all the doors and windows, peering out at every car that passes by."

"I live alone in an apartment in the city. I don't think I would feel insecure here. My home, where my parents live, is on the outskirts of a small town, so I'm accustomed to not having any close neighbors," Kathleen replied. "Is M— your father away a great deal?"

"More often gone than he's here," Annette replied nonchalantly, as if it was a fact she had become accustomed to a long time ago. "You see, he works for an oil company. He's a troubleshooter, and they send him wherever they're having problems. Sometimes he's gone for a week and sometimes months. He's somewhere in the Middle East now."

"He's traveled all over the world," Marsha inserted with a faint air of pride.

"Do you girls ever go with him?" Kathleen tipped her dark auburn head on one side curiously.

"We used to—during summer vacations," Annette answered.

"And holidays. We never spend a holiday apart," Marsha rushed to assure her. "If daddy is away for Christmas or Easter or Thanksgiving or our birthdays, we always fly to wherever he is to celebrate with him. It isn't fair for him to always spend them alone. I mean, Annette and I have each other."

Blinking her hazel eyes in astonishment, Kathleen had been about to feel sorry for the two girls who were so constantly left alone by their father. They were more concerned for him. Marsha's lack of selfishness surprised her, and she sensed that the younger sister was without guile.

"What about summer?" Kathleen questioned. "You don't spend it with him any more?"

"Oh, yes," Annette nodded decisively. "He arranges his vacation to be with us."

"One year the company had a really bad problem and they tried to persuade daddy to cut his vacation short, but he wouldn't do it. He said if it was really bad, it would wait until he came back to work and if it wasn't, they would solve it themselves without him." Marsha sat forward on her chair.

"Actually he did help," the older sister corrected with marked patience. "He made a lot of telephone calls and consulted for days with the man the company sent out. He just didn't go himself. Now—" she breathed in deeply "—the agency did explain that you would do the cooking and all but the major cleaning. We have a woman who comes once a week for that. Marsha and I take care of our own rooms and help with the other stuff."

"That was explained to me," Kathleen said, silently marveling at the adept way the girl switched the topic away from her father.

11

"Actually—may I call you Kathleen?" At Kathleen's nod, Annette continued, "Actually, Kathleen, I think the three of us will get along very well. We'll give Aunt Helen a copy of the application the agency supplied, as well as our endorsement of you. I can't think of any more questions we need to ask."

The interview was obviously being concluded. Kathleen had thought she would see Mrs. Long before she left, but that evidently was not the case. It seemed unusual that an ultimate decision would be reached without her having ever spoken to an adult of the family.

"Annette!" The voice calling from the hallway raised an octave on the last syllable.

'The girl winced visibly while Marsha murmured in a low groan, "Aunt Helen!"

2

nnette recovered swiftly, smiling at Kathleen with commendable aplomb. "That will be our aunt. She'll see you now." She turned to her sister, the angle of her pivot concealing much of her expression from Kathleen. "Marsha, let Aunt Helen know we're in here."

With obvious reluctance, the other girl slid to her feet, her blue eyes glancing uncertainly at Kathleen. Noiselessly she hurried over the carpet to the hall door. The door remained partially ajar as she stepped through, allowing the older woman's voice to carry clearly into the study.

"There you are. Is your sister with you, Marsha?"

Marsha's answer couldn't be heard, her voice sounding as only a low murmur. The aunt's response made it evident that she had been informed of Kathleen's presence.

"And you girls have been entertaining her? That was very thoughtful."

As the door opened, Kathleen rose to her feet. Respect and deference to her elders had been ingrained in her since childhood, a simple matter of good manners, her parents insisted. Either way, it was a habit she had continued in her adult years. A large woman followed Marsha into the study. She was not tall as much as she was plumply overweight, in her early sixties, perhaps. She wore a string of pearls around her throat and her blue flowered dress intensified the blue rinse she used in her gray hair. She moved slowly as if walking was difficult for her.

A glance at the swollen joints of her fingers indicated to Kathleen that the woman suffered from arthritis. It probably plagued the joints of her legs, too. The extra weight no doubt aggravated the condition. She understood more fully why the woman didn't feel capable of keeping up with two active girls. There were probably mornings when it was a chore to get out of bed.

"Aunt Helen—" Annette came forward "—this is Kathleen Darrow. The employment agency sent her out. This is our great-aunt, Mrs. Helen Long."

"How do you do, Mrs. Long." Kathleen offered her hand in greeting. It was held briefly and released.

A pair of friendly but keen blue eyes swept over her. Mental notes were made by the woman of the rusty highlights in Kathleen's brown hair, her expressive hazel eyes with their green sparkle beneath a fringe of dark lashes, the strong cheekbones and straight nose, the fulsome curve of her mouth into a dimpling smile and the generous female curves of her figure beneath the rust-brown suit.

"I hope I haven't kept you waiting too long, Miss Darrow." The older woman smiled at her politely.

Absently Kathleen glanced at her watch, prepared to say she had only been there a few minutes, but her interview with the girls had consumed the better part of half an hour.

"Not very long," she replied, choosing an indefinite reply instead.

"I hope not," Helen Long answered sincerely. "I should hate to have you make the trip all the way out here and wait for me as well. Especially—" she paused and Kathleen noticed Annette's mouth tightening into a grim line"— well, the agency did warn me that they were sending out someone who was younger than Jordan—Mr. Long—had requested. I presumed they meant someone in her thirties. But you, Miss Darrow, you can't be more than—" There was an expressive lift of her hand.

And Kathleen filled in the blank. "I'm twenty-five, Mrs. Long."

The woman sighed, indicating that her answer had settled the matter. "I'm so sorry you made the trip all the way out here for nothing, but we really must have someone older for the job. I feel that it's my fault for not inquiring more fully when the girl from the agency phoned."

"It's quite all right. I understand," Kathleen assured her, but her mind was racing.

A few minutes ago Annette had all but promised the job would be hers, that age was not a problem at all. Now, neither girl was saying a word, just standing silently beside their great-aunt. She was crazy to have believed them

14

even for an instant. It was just that, after meeting the girls and seeing the home, Kathleen would have liked to have had the job.

"May I offer you some tea or coffee?" Mrs. Long murmured apologetically.

"No, thank you. I really must be going," Kathleen refused gently. Glancing at the two girls, she smiled. "I enjoyed meeting both of you. Maybe we'll run into each other again some time."

Covertly Marsha slid a look at her sister behind her aunt's back, her expression resigned and defeated. Annette's pointed chin raised a fraction of an inch. Her smoke-colored eyes were clear and implacable.

"We enjoyed meeting you, Miss Darrow," she responded. "I'll walk with you to the door."

There was a brief exchange of goodbyes and another apology from Mrs. Long for Kathleen's abortive trip, then she was walking into the entry hall toward the front door.

"I wouldn't worry about the job, Kathleen," said Annette, reverting casually to her first name. "Marsha and I will talk Aunt Helen around to our way of thinking." She made the statement with all the certainty of the very young. "You know how it is when a person gets old. Everyone under thirty is a juvenile to them."

"Mrs. Long seemed very definite," Kathleen cautioned. She had accepted the decision as final and hoped the girls would, too. It was better that they didn't count too heavily on changing their great-aunt's mind.

"You do want to come here and live, don't you? With us?" The gray eyes stared unwaveringly at her.

Pausing at the front door, Kathleen considered her words carefully before answering. "I think it would have been enjoyable and the three of us would have probably gotten along quite well, as you said, but I'm sure Mrs. Long will find someone older, and someone that you girls will get along with just as well."

"Trust us," Annette declared earnestly. "If we can't get around Aunt Helen—well, the final decision rests with dad. He'll listen to us. Would you promise not to take another job until you've heard definitely one way or the other?"

Biting into her lower lip, Kathleen hesitated. "I have to find work. I can't wait very long."

"Two weeks. Give us two weeks."

There was something about Annette's attitude. She wasn't imploring Kathleen to wait; she was just positively confident that Kathleen couldn't ignore the request. What was she doing…listening to a twelve-year-old?

"All right, two weeks." The concession was made before Kathleen realized what she was saying. She resigned herself to abiding by the promise.

15

Two weeks wasn't so very long. Despite the young girl's optimism, Kathleen didn't believe she would be offered the position. Mrs. Long had been definite and she was carrying out her nephew's instructions.

"You'll hear from us," Annette promised with a satisfied smile spreading across her face. Mrs. Long stepped out of the study and the blond girl slipped a politely bland mask over her expression. "It was nice meeting you, Miss Darrow."

As Kathleen walked to her little Volkswagen, she didn't attempt to suppress the smile that surfaced. She liked the two girls, but she also realized that to stay ahead of them, a person would have to be on their toes all the time. More so when it came to Annette than Marsha. Annette was the leader and Marsha was the follower. They were a formidable pair, but no doubt their father and their great-aunt were fully aware of it.

CLOSING THE DOOR, Annette pivoted toward her sister and great-aunt, an expression of careless unconcern on her face. Long, lighthearted steps carried her past them to the closed stairwell door in the hall.

"I'm going up to my room to listen to some records," she declared. "Are you coming, Marsha?" At her sister's nod of agreement, Annette paused at the door. "You'll be watching your soap opera, won't you, Aunt Helen?"

"Yes, I suppose so. Why?" The woman blinked curiously.

"Oh—" the girl lifted her shoulders in an expressive movement" —I just wanted to know. If you're watching television, I didn't want to turn the stereo up too loud. Come on, Marsha."

Annette took the steps two at a time, not pausing until she had reached her room and Marsha had closed the door. She flopped onto the bed, signaling her younger sister to put a record on the stereo. As the sensual beat of a rock tune filled the room, Marsha joined her on the bed, sitting cross-legged near the foot.

She sighed heavily. "What are we going to do now, 'Nette?"

Annette was sprawled crossways on the bed on her stomach, her fingers drumming the floor in time with the music.

She straightened partially to lean her elbows on the bed. "We'll simply have to revise our plan, that's all," Annette shrugged. "We might as well start now. You sneak downstairs and get her application so I can start tracing it onto the blank form."

"Did you really like her?" Marsha frowned anxiously.

"Yes." Annette rolled onto her side, supremely confident and self-assured. "I always know within minutes of meeting someone whether I'm going to like them or not. You have to admit she was friendly and not overbearing. What choice do we have, anyway? You know Helen is going to recommend the

16

'dragon lady'." Marsha grimaced. "If we want to have any say in the matter of who lives with us, we're going to have to take things in our own hands."

"But she's so young," Marsha persisted with her doubts. "How are you going to change her age on the paper without getting caught?"

"Simple. I'll just invert the numbers of the year she was born. It will look like an inadvertent mistake. Now go downstairs and get the application from the study desk. And don't let Helen catch you."

Marsha shook her head. She had considerably more misgivings about the plan than her older sister had. "Are you sure we're doing the right thing?"

"Sooner or later dad is going to find out about it," Annette acknowledged with blissful unconcern. "But once it's done, it's not so easily undone. You'll see!"

KATHLEEN DIDN'T RELATE the full details of her interview to Barry or her friends. All she told them was that she didn't think she would be offered the job. She didn't mention her promise not to accept another position. It became more absurd the more she thought about it.

Still, when she was offered a well-paid job the following Tuesday as an adviser to a firm that designed uniforms for the medical profession, Kathleen asked for time to consider her acceptance. It was granted since the job would involve moving out of state, something she would be reluctant to do in any case. She chided herself for being foolish enough to give the promise in the first place. If she lost an interesting and challenging job because of it, there would be no one to blame but herself.

The employment agency supplied her with appointments for several more job interviews. Fortunately, none of them were what she was looking for and only one company tentatively offered her a job.

"DO YOU HAVE THE ENVELOPE?" Marsha whispered as Annette tiptoed through the hall door into the kitchen.

With a grin of triumph, Annette held up the thick manilla envelope and carefully closed the door behind her. "Has the water started to boil yet?"

"No." Brown curls danced about her neck as Marsha shook her head.

"For heaven's sake, dummy!" Annette exclaimed in a hissing whisper. "Hold the lid back on the teakettle or it'll whistle when it starts boiling. It might wake Helen, and she'll come in here to find out what we're doing."

"It's too hot to try to hold it back," Marsha defended.

"Well, tie it hack with a string or something. There's some in the catchall drawer, I think." With the lid of the teakettle haphazardly tied open, steam began to rise. "The envelope flap is already partially unsealed. It shouldn't take much to steam it the rest of the way open."

Annette's tongue darted out one corner of her mouth as she concentrated on exposing the partially sealed envelope flap to the rising steam. Her fingers kept dancing along the edge of the thick envelope to avoid prolonged exposure to the burning heat. Marsha picked up the two sheets of paper lying on the counter.

"You really did a neat job, Annette," she murmured. "I can hardly tell which is the original and which is the one you did."

"All I had to do was trace over her handwriting and make the changes we wanted. Just don't get them mixed up and stick the wrong one in the envelope," Annette warned with a frown. Her prying fingers lifted the flap, its sealing glue loosened by the steam. "There, I've got it!"

Taming off the fire beneath the kettle, she quickly withdrew the contents of the envelope. Marsha handed her the completed application form, but Annette checked it to be certain it was the right one. She slid it in the middle of the other forms.

"Now for Helen's letter," she breathed out slowly. "Thank goodness, she typed it! I wasn't looking forward to trying to trace her scrawling scratch. Her arthritis must have been bothering her. All I'll have to worry about is the signature, which will be a snap!" Annette quickly skimmed the contents. "She recommended the dragon lady to dad. Ugh! Helen doesn't know it, but—" her gray eyes sparkled wickedly "—she's about to recommend Miss Kathleen Darrow as well."

"You aren't going to leave the dragon lady's name in there, are you?" Marsha moaned. "She'd be sending us to bed at eight o'clock every night."

"I have to leave her in. She sounds so highly qualified and experienced that dad would be suspicious if Helen didn't comment on her," Annette explained impatiently. She set her great-aunt's letter to one side and removed several folded sheets of paper from the pocket of her slacks. "I wrote dad a letter, too. In the beginning, it's just stuff about us, but here's the way I signed it off. 'I thought I'd let you know what Marsha and I thought about the women who applied for the job. All of them were all right, but we thought the nicest one was Miss Darrow. We can hardly wait until you come home.' Etcetera. That, combined with Helen's mention of her, should do the trick. Do you have some sheets of Helen's stationery?"

"It's right here." Marsha pointed to the floral bordered paper on the breakfast table. "How soon will daddy get this?"

"Helen's taking us into town tomorrow morning and dropping the envelope off at the company office. One of their planes is leaving tomorrow afternoon, so dad will have this as soon as the plane gets there. With luck, he'll send word or call to hire Kathleen," she replied, crossing her fingers.

"But what if Aunt Helen says something about her being so young?"

"You know how Helen is," Annette sighed. "She isn't about to argue with daddy. She has terribly old-fashioned notions about men making the decisions."

"I hope you're right," was the doubting response.

"Oh, Marsha, you're such an alarmist!" Annette declared with a disparaging roll of her eyes. "Bring the envelope and come with me to the study. I'm glad Helen types nearly as badly as she writes. I won't have to worry so much about mistakes."

"All of this seems so underhanded and sneaky," Marsha whispered as Annette peered around the kitchen door, listening for some sound of their great-aunt's stirring.

"Well, of course it's sneaky," Annette hissed, shaking her head hopelessly. Her younger sister had absolutely no sense of adventure!

THE CHAIR TEETERED SLIGHTLY, and Kathleen grasped the back of it to regain her balance. Using the closet shelf for support, she again tried to reach the box at the far end of the shelf. Her fingertips brushed it, but she couldn't stretch far enough to reach it.

"How on earth did I get it in there?" she muttered aloud to herself.

Straightening, with her hands on her hips, she surveyed the situation again from her stand on top of the chrome chair from the breakfast set. The sleeves of her bulky gray sweatshirt were pushed back to her elbows. A blue scarf kept her auburn hair away from her face. Below the snug-fitting blue jeans, her feet were bare.

"If I could remember what was in that stupid box, I wouldn't have to go through this," she sighed.

Her gaze fell on a wire hanger. Reaching for it, she decided to try to hook the box and pull it closer until she could reach it. But before she could find out if her plan would work, the apartment doorbell rang. With a frustrated sigh, she hopped down from the chair, tossing the hanger among the cluttered pile of discards on her bed.

Saturday afternoon had seemed such a perfect time to clean out the closets, a task she had been meaning to do for the last two years. But all she had was one interruption on top of another. Maggie had phoned, then her mother. Some salesman selling vacuum cleaners had appeared at her doorstep and Kathleen had thought she would never get rid of him.

Her hand paused on the doorknob. "Who is it?" If it was that salesman again, she had no intention of opening the door.

"It's me, Barry."

In double quick time, she unlocked the door and flung it open. "You're a lifesaver!" She grabbed his hand and without a word of explanation led him into the small bedroom of her flat.

"It looks as if a cyclone went through here," he commented.

"One called hurricane Kathleen," she laughed, pausing at the closet. "I can't reach that box on the top shelf. Will you get it down for me?"

"Sure." Obligingly, he reached up, his taller height enabling him to reach it without the aid of a chair. "What are you doing?"

"Mercilessly going through closets and drawers and getting rid of everything I don't wear or use any more." She knelt beside the box as he set it on the floor. "I can't believe the way things accumulate in such a short time."

"Things don't accumulate," Barry corrected with a good-natured smile. "People accumulate things."

"That's true." Kathleen opened the box flaps to view the contents. "My high-school scrapbook!" she exclaimed, then, "my photograph album and my collection of paper dolls. I thought all of this was stored in the attic at home." She put everything back, resisting the impulse to go through it, and closed the flap. "I guess you can put it back on the shelf, only not so far that I can't reach it this time."

Her intention to supervise the replacement of the box was denied by the jarring ring of the telephone in the living room. Grumbling at the constant interruptions, she hurried to answer it.

She picked up the beige receiver on the fourth ring. "Kathleen Darrow speaking." She used her crisp professional voice that had always succeeded in bullying recalcitrant patients into taking their medicine.

"Your party is on the line, sir," an operator spoke.

A brown eyebrow shot up. Long-distance? Who could possibly be telephoning her long-distance? And why? Her first thought was that there had been an accident at home.

"Miss Darrow, Jordan Long calling." The male voice was brusque and low-pitched, yet oddly pleasing in a manly sort of way.

"Yes?" The name was familiar, but for an instant she couldn't place it. She would surely have remembered hearing that voice before if she knew him.

He must have caught the questioning blankness in her tone. "That's the Kathleen Darrow who applied for the position in my home looking after my daughters?"

"Yes, Mr. Long." The name fell into place. "I'm sorry, but my first reaction when I realized this was a long-distance call was that it was bad news about someone in my family."

"Of course." The voice smoothly dismissed her explanation as unimportant. "My aunt, Mrs. Long, forwarded me your application and list of references. You seem to be regarded as a highly responsible and sensible woman. My daughters also seem to like you."

"We did have a lengthy talk," Kathleen acknowledged, still trying to take in the fact that he had actually called her. Annette had said that they would let her know one way or the other about the job.

"Would you be able to start on Monday? My aunt will stay for a few days until you settle in."

There was a chair nearby and Kathleen gratefully sank onto it. "Do you mean you're offering me the job?" Her training as a nurse had schooled her well. Very little of her surprise crept into her voice as she requested a clarification of his statement.

"Yes," was the clipped answer. Then he asked, "You are still interested in the position?"

"Yes, but—"Her teeth sank quickly into her lip. She had been about to question him on the age requirement that he had indicated to his aunt, but it was foolish to look a gift horse in the mouth.

She wanted the job, and he had obviously looked into her background and been satisfied that she was capable.

"Is there something wrong, Miss Darrow?" The piercing quietness of his voice seemed to cross the miles to pin her down.

Kathleen cast aside her uncertainty. "Not at all, Mr. Long," she answered smoothly. "I was merely considering all the packing and arrangements regarding my apartment that I would need to make before Monday. With the exception of one or two items that can be handled by telephone, I should be ready to start on Monday." It would mean racing around madly, but she could do it.

"You are familiar with the salary arrangements and your free time?"

"Yes."

"Mrs. Long will go over the household budget with you and any other domestic details you'll need to know. I'll let her know she can expect you some time on Monday." His abruptness was slightly unnerving.

"Am I allowed to have friends over occasionally to spend an evening or an afternoon with me?" Kathleen asked.

"I don't see why it wouldn't be permissible occasionally," Jordan Long agreed blandly. "Is there anything else?"

"I don't believe so. If any other questions arise I'm sure I'll be able to obtain the necessary answers from Mrs. Long," Kathleen replied.

"Very well. It will be another two weeks or so before I'm back in the States. I'll look forward to meeting you in person then, Miss Darrow." It was a rather polite statement.

"Thank you. So will I," she replied, with a bit more sincerity than politeness in her comment, since she was curious to know what the man looked like who belonged to that voice.

The thought made her smile as the line went dead. The last time she had been curious about a man's voice, she had been sorely disappointed when she met him. The sexy male voice that had called the hospital every day for a

21

week inquiring about a patient on Kathleen's floor had belonged to a man who looked like a stork, all arms and logs and a beaky nose.

"Who is Mr. Long?" Barry's voice surprised Kathleen as she replaced the beige receiver in its cradle.

She turned slightly to see him standing in the bedroom doorway. She had completely forgotten he was there. His attention was curiously focused on the bemused smile curving her lips.

"Do you remember the job I was interviewed for last week, taking care of two girls?" she asked. Barry nodded. "Well, I've just been offered it."

"I thought you said you weren't even being considered," he frowned.

"I thought I wasn't," she said, shrugging her shoulders to communicate her own surprise. "I guess it simply proves you should never underestimate the power of a child. The oldest girl, Annette, said I would get the job as I was leaving," she explained, "even though the aunt flatly told me I was too young. It seems the father put more stock in his daughters' wishes than his aunt's opinion. I start Monday."

"You accepted?" Barry didn't look very pleased at the announcement.

"Yes, I did," she stated positively. She suddenly realized all the things she had to do before Monday. She walked briskly toward the bedroom. "Wait until you meet the girls, Barry," she began chatting, dragging an empty box to the middle of the room. "The oldest is blond and fair with big gray eyes. Her sister is dark with blue eyes. A complete contrast—an angel and a devil, but I think the roles are reversed. You'll like them, I know."

"ANNETTE AND MARSHA! Your father is on the telephone!" Helen Long called up the staircase. "He wants to talk to you!"

"This is it!" Annette hissed excitedly as she and her sister tumbled out of her room and charged down the steps. "Now we'll find out if our plan worked. Let me talk first."

In the living room, Annette quickly took the telephone receiver from her great-aunt's hand while Marsha shifted nervously beside her. Taking a deep breath, she met her sister's anxious look. Two of the fingers holding the telephone receiver were crossed.

"Hello, dad! How are you?" she said brightly. "You usually only call on Sundays. What's up? Are you coming home sooner than you thought?" She winked an eye at Marsha as she bit a corner of her lip.

"I'm afraid not," Jordan Long replied. His voice wasn't brusque, but warmly indulgent instead. "I phoned to let Aunt Helen know I've decided on someone to take her place."

"Oh? Who?" Annette tried to make her voice sound mildly interested, but her heart was jumping all over the place.

22

"The one you girls seemed to prefer, Kathleen Darrow."

A grin of triumph split Annette's face as she gave Marsha the thumbs up sign of victory. "Oh, yes, she was nice," she said, suppressing the urge to giggle and keeping her back turned to Helen Long. "Aunt Helen can phone her this afternoon to let her know."

"That won't be necessary." There was a crackle of interference on the line and Annette only managed to understand the last part of his statement. "— Talk to her myself."

"There's no need for you to talk to her, dad," she rushed. Panic sprang into Marsha's blue eyes as she listened to only one side of the conversation. "We can call her just as easily from here."

"I said I've already talked to her," he repeated with amused patience. "She'll be there on Monday."

"You've already talked to her?" Annette repeated slowly, swallowing tightly as she wound the receiver cord nervously in her fingers. "What did she say?"

"Nothing very much. She accepted the job and said she would be there on Monday."

"What did you think of her?" She held her breath, her gaze locked to her younger sister's.

"She seems well qualified." There was an underlying current of curiosity in his tone and Annette quickly heeded the warning that she was asking too many questions about his reaction to Kathleen.

"Yes, well, I suppose so," she agreed indifferently, and launched into a falsely enthusiastic account of the things they had been doing the past few days. By the time she handed the telephone to Marsha whatever suspicions he might have had were forgotten.

"That was a close one," Annette sighed when she and Marsha were once again in her upstairs bedroom. "I never dreamed daddy might call to talk to her himself. Thank heavens it's hard to judge a person's age just by their voice, or our plans would have gone down the drain."

"He isn't going to be happy when he finds out," Marsha reminded her.

"Will you stop being such a worry wart!" Annette exclaimed impatiently. "We'll cross that bridge when we come to it."

3

There hadn't really been much settling in for Kathleen to do. Almost from the minute her clothes were unpacked and hung in the closet, she had felt at home. She had been given an upstairs bedroom near the two that the girls used. Helen had used the room off the kitchen, originally the cook's quarters, because it was so difficult for her to go up and down stairs.

Surprisingly, the girls were very domestically inclined, especially when it came to cooking. They loved to experiment in the kitchen, trying new dishes. Between them and Helen Long, Kathleen had quickly become familiar with where everything was.

When it came time for Helen to move back into her small bungalow in town, the four of them made almost a party of the task. Kathleen had been given the keys to the Continental in the garage, but she had felt more at ease using her Volkswagen to transport Helen's belongings.

With everyone and everything squashed into the small car, Annette's remark that she felt like a sardine had set the humorous and happy note for the moving. And the tone didn't change all through the unpacking and putting away.

With Helen Long's departure, the girls became less inhibited. More activities and Outings were suggested now that they were not restricted by the older woman's limited physical capacity. Not that Kathleen spent most of her time chauffeuring the girls around. They were accustomed to entertaining themselves.

At the close of her first week, Kathleen decided things were working out better than she could have hoped. The girls squabbled between themselves every now and then, sometimes jointly testing her will, but mostly they regarded Kathleen as a big sister with authority.

The last of the Sunday dinner dishes were cleared away, and Kathleen wandered into the living room. Marsha was standing at one of the windows, gazing silently through the panes. Annette was slouched in one of the large cushioned chairs, a leg dangling over one of the arms while she flipped through the pages of a movie magazine.

"It's a beautiful day," Kathleen commented, glancing curiously from one to the other as she sensed the vague restlessness in the air. "Why aren't you outside?"

Annette closed the magazine and tossed it onto the coffee table, then slouched deeper in the chair, swinging her leg in the air. "Father always calls on Sunday."

On cue, the telephone rang and Annette jumped up from her chair to answer. After her initial hello, her gaze shifted to Kathleen and she held out the phone to her.

"It's for you," she announced, her lips compressed in a line of impatient resignation. "A man."

Kathleen took the receiver and Annette slumped into her chair again, with Marsha taking up a position behind it. "Hello," Kathleen answered, guessing even before she received a reply that the only man who could be calling would be Barry.

"Hi." She was right, it was Barry. "I thought I would phone to see how you were doing."

"Fine, just fine," she replied. The last time she had talked to him, Helen had still been living with them. She hadn't yet taken advantage of Mr. Long's permission to have visitors. She had decided to wait until her footing with the girls was sounder.

"Do you have anything planned for this afternoon? I thought I could drive out and take you and the girls to the beach," Barry suggested.

"Maybe another time." Kathleen glanced at Annette, who was absently chewing her lower lip. "Do you mind if I phone you later, Barry? The girls are waiting for an overseas call from their father."

"No, no, I don't mind," he agreed, but with an underlying tone of reluctance.

"I'll talk to you later," she promised. "'Bye!"

His goodbye sounded into the room as Kathleen was already starting to replace the receiver in its cradle. She walked to the green and yellow print sofa, its airy spring colors repeated in the decor of the rest of the room.

"Was that your boyfriend?" Marsha asked.

Kathleen checked the impulse to explain the slightly platonic relationship she had with Barry and merely nodded. "Yes. His name is Barry Manning."

"Do you like him very much?" Annette gave her a considering look, the expression in her gray eyes unreadable.

"Yes, he's very nice," Kathleen answered truthfully.

"What does he do?" Marsha tipped her head on one side, a wing of curling dark hair falling across her cheek.

"He sells insurance."

"Is he very handsome?"

Before Kathleen could answer Annette's question, the telephone rang again—which was just as well, because she hadn't a clue as to how to describe Barry. She had never considered his looks all that much.

Annette's quick speech into the telephone was followed immediately by, "Hi, dad, how are you?" and Marsha moved quickly to her side, not displaying as much excitement as her older sister.

"This Friday! You're coming home this Friday!" Annette exclaimed. There was a long pause during which Annette seemed to hold herself motionless. When next she spoke, it was with false enthusiasm. "Oh, no, it sounds like a fine idea. I was—just thinking about Marsha, that's all." She twisted her fingers in the coil of the receiver cord. With a slight pivot, she turned her back toward Kathleen. "Well, you know how she is about flying. I mean, maybe it would be better if we postponed it until you're home and we can drive over there for a couple of days...Who? Miss Darrow?"

Annette's back visibly stiffened and Marsha's eyes widened apprehensively. "Oh, I don't think so, dad, I mean...Yes, all right," came the grudging agreement.

The squared shoulders turned, a bland expression on Annette's face as she looked at Kathleen. "Father wants to talk to you."

Kathleen walked to the telephone. Crazily, her palms were sweating, although there was no reason for her to be nervous. She wiped them dry in a smoothing motion over the thigh portion of her slacks. There was something in the offing that she sensed Annette didn't like, a trip of some sort.

"Yes, Mr. Long?" She spoke with professional crispness into the phone.

"Hello, Miss Darrow. Are you settling in all right?" The low pitch of his voice was the same, but it lacked the brusqueness of their previous conversation. Its friendly interest made it all the more pleasing, and Kathleen felt herself warming to its sound.

"Very well. I feel practically at home," she admitted. "I overheard Annette say something about you returning this coming Friday."

"I'll be flying into Washington, D.C. on Friday," Jordan Long explained. "I've been promising the girls a tour of the capital for several years, and I decided this would be an opportune time to keep the promise."

"I see. You're going to have the girls fly in to meet you." Her hazel eyes shifted to the two girls listening intently to her conversation.

"Yes," came the agreeing reply. "Have you ever been to Washington, Miss Darrow?"

"Some time ago," Kathleen admitted. "My parents took me and my brothers and sisters when I was sixteen."

"Then you'll enjoy seeing it again as much as the girls." Before Kathleen could comment, he continued, "Marsha doesn't take to flying very well—she's invariably airsick. I would like you to come with them."

"I'll be happy to." At long last she would meet the man who belonged to this rather sensual voice. Then she concentrated her thoughts on the details of the trip. "How long will we stay there?"

"Over the weekend. We'll leave on Monday afternoon. I've taken care of the hotel and plane reservations and arranged for you to pick up your tickets at the airline counter."

He gave her the name of the airline, the flight number and its departure time. Kathleen quickly jotted the information down on the message pad beside the telephone. Afterwards Jordan Long asked to speak to his youngest daughter, Marsha.

It was a short conversation. Almost the instant that Marsha hung up the telephone, Annette was taking her by the arm and hurriedly leading her away.

"Come on, Marsha," she ordered. "Let's go and pick out the clothes we're going to take on the trip."

Kathleen watched them rush toward the stairs. A faint smile touched her mouth. There certainly wasn't any of the lingering reluctance toward the trip that Annette had expressed initially.

As a matter of fact, Kathleen's thoughts were running along the same lines. What clothes would she pack for herself?

ANNETTE SWEPT INTO HER BEDROOM, angry frustration glittering in her silver-gray eyes. She grabbed the bright throw pillow from the top of her bed and crushed it against her stomach as she spun around to sit on the bed.

"Why did he have to do it?" she demanded of the silent Marsha. "Why? Why? Why?" The slam of the pillow against the soft bed punctuated each question. "All of our strategy has just been thrown out the window!"

With the explosion released, Annette rose to her feet and began pacing the room, the pillow still in hand. She nibbled at her lower lip, deep in concentration.

"What are we going to do?" Marsha asked urgently.

"I'm thinking!"

FRIDAY MORNING found Kathleen scurrying around the house dusting and cleaning, trying to make each room neat as a pin. She had just put fresh sheets on the large bed in the master bedroom and was smoothing the beige coverlet over the top.

The shag carpet of chocolate brown was thick and soft beneath her bare feet. She liked this room, she decided as she glanced around it again. The walls were an ivory beige with walnut woodwork. Drapes, the same shade as the bedspread, hung at the windows with insets of brown sheers. The walnut furniture was bulky and solid, befitting the masculine aura of the room. A cushioned armchair sat in one corner of the room with a reading lamp beside it. It was a cozy touch that kept the room from being malely austere.

A louvered walk-in closet took up nearly one whole wall of the room. Kathleen had inspected it quite unashamedly during her first week at the house. There were a few clothes in it, shirts, slacks and suits, some shoes. She had guessed that Jordan Long had taken the majority of his wardrobe with him.

The clothes had told her one thing about him, though. He was neither short nor fat and had excellent taste. Except for more casual wear, his suits were all expensively tailored—a fact that didn't surprise Kathleen since she had already noticed that the clothes the girls wore were sensibly not expensive but made of quality material and workmanship just the same.

Kathleen still wondered about the absence of photographs in the bedroom. There were several in the study, all of them of Annette and Marsha. She had not seen any of Jordan Long or of his wife who, Kathleen had learned, died when Marsha was three. Neither of the girls had seemed inclined to discuss her further and Kathleen had stifled her natural curiosity.

Both girls talked often about their father, yet mostly relating episodes that involved the three of them together. Kathleen learned little about what manner of man he was, except that he seemed quite fond of his children and dedicated to his job, circumstances that created an involuntary conflict.

In spite of the many days he spent away from his children, they didn't appear to resent it. So Kathleen decided they had successfully resolved the separation of interests.

A sigh caught in her throat. She didn't really have time for this curious contemplation about her employer. There was still lunch to get ready, and she wanted to shower before changing into the ivory linen suit she had decided to wear for the short plane journey. She had supervised the packing of their suitcases yesterday, minus the last-minute items. Both girls had been cognizant of the various types of outfits they would need to take, revealing a travel experience that far outstripped Kathleen's.

Thinking about the girls made Kathleen realize that although they were quite normal in many respects, they were remarkable. She doubted that the credit belonged to her predecessor, whoever that was, or to Helen Long. All the roads seemed to lead back to her employer, and late this afternoon she would finally be meeting him face to face.

PUSHING MARSHA AHEAD OF HER, Annette slipped into the aisle of the plane ahead of several other disembarking passengers. Kathleen was not quick enough unstrapping her seatbelt to fall in behind them and lagged two passengers back, as Annette had planned.

"Remember what I told you," she whispered fiercely in Marsha's ear, her face looking even paler against her dark hair. "Depending on which way dad reacts we'll decide which plan we use. If he looks angry when he sees Kathleen—you know, that icy-cold look when he's really mad—then we'll nonchalantly begin talking about the things we've been doing, indicating indirectly how well we're getting along with Kathleen. But for heaven's sake, Marsha, don't pour it on too thick!"

"Okay," Marsha nodded lethargically, a result of the motion-sickness pill she had taken before the flight's departure.

Annette's hand closed over Marsha's shoulder. "We'll wait for Kathleen here." She guided her sister between two seats to let the departing passengers by, then joined in the line in front of Kathleen.

"STAY CLOSE, GIRLS," Kathleen warned as they emerged from the plane. "I don't want to lose one of you in the crowd."

After she had said it, she wished she hadn't even voiced the nightmarish idea. Here she was, anxious to impress her employer. Imagine what it would be like confronting him with the fact that one of his daughters had strayed away from her! Kathleen shuddered. That would not be the way to make a good first impression.

In the last three hours, Kathleen had had little time to dwell on her coming meeting with Jordan Long. First there had been the locking up of the house and making sure nothing had been left behind, then driving to the airport, picking up the tickets, boarding the plane, and soothing Marsha's anxious nerves during the flight. Now she could feel the tingle of anticipation begin.

According to the timetable Jordan Long had supplied to her, his flight should have arrived an hour earlier. Somewhere in the terminal area of the international airport, he would be waiting for them. Kathleen wished for an opportunity to freshen up, but she could tell by the rather tense expressions on the girls' faces that they were anxious to see their father. Who could blame them for being so eager to be with him after their long separation?

Leaving the plane walkway, they entered the small waiting area of the flight gate. Annette breathed in sharply and hesitated a step before breaking into a wide smile.

"There he is!" She dashed from Kathleen's side with a just as exuberant Marsha following seconds later.

It was a moment before Kathleen was able to discern who of the many strangers was the object of their attention. Then her gaze separated the man in a summer checked suit and white shirt from the rest of the men in the crowd.

She had a brief impression of height, somewhere around six feet, before he bent toward the two girls rushing toward him. Thick black hair was brushed carelessly across his forehead. There was a tendency for it to wave at the ends. His face, boldly and ruggedly carved in blatantly masculine features, had been browned by exposure to the sun. There was a dimpling cleft in his chin that seemed to deepen as he smiled, which he was doing now.

Strong arms encircled the two girls hugging him. The open happiness and affection that was being displayed by the three was a beautiful thing to see. Kathleen discovered there was a lump forming in her throat at the sight. Years of training enabled her to swallow it away as she walked slowly toward them, giving them the time to enjoy a private reunion.

Before she reached them, Jordan Long's gaze focused on her, running over her curves in assessing approval. Kathleen's confidence grew. The three afternoons she had spent at the beach with the girls had brought a golden tint to her skin which the ivory suit set off to perfection. The sheer fabric of her blouse was in vibrant greens and golds, intensifying the glitter of green in her eyes and the shimmer of fire in her hair.

Several steps closer, Kathleen was able to distinguish the color of his eyes. They were charcoal gray, outlined with thick ebony lashes. The impression of black smoke was all the more apparent because of the searing warmth in his gaze of masculine admiration. Her heart skipped a beat as the smile on his well-formed mouth was directed at her. She responded to it with a dimpling one of her own.

Then his attention flickered to the girls and Kathleen heard him say, "And where is the redoubtable Miss Darrow? You didn't shove her out of the plane, did you?"

"Oh, dad!" Annette laughed, but it was a rather anxious look she shot over her shoulder to ascertain Kathleen's approach. "Here she comes now," she answered.

The smile had faded slightly on Kathleen's face. Since she had realized who he was, she had automatically assumed that Jordan Long had guessed her identity when he had smiled at her. The discovery that his attention had been solely that of a virile man admiring an attractive woman caught her off guard.

His gaze flickered past Kathleen, then returned with lightning swiftness as the fact registered that she was the only woman in the vicinity. The black smoke of his eyes dissipated into shards of cold steel. For a split second Kathleen faltered, then recovered her poise to walk the last few feet to the group.

"You are Kathleen Darrow?" Shavings of ice ran through his voice as he made the accusation.

Forced by his superior height to tip her head back to look into his face, Kathleen felt intimidated, but she had faced too many head nurses, doctors and irate relatives to let it show.

"That's correct," she answered pleasantly. Her mind raced, trying to find the cause for this sudden switch from approval to icy displeasure. "It's a pleasure to finally meet you, Mr. Long."

She offered a hand in greeting and received a short but punishing grip from his tanned fingers. There was a harsh, sardonic twist to his mouth.

"I'm sure it is," he responded in a voice as dry and unwelcoming as a desert wind.

Kathleen had the uncomfortable sensation that there were several more scathing comments he intended to make.

Fortunately Annette chose that moment to give him another quick hug.

"It's so good to have you back, dad," Annette sighed. "We thought we'd have to search all over the terminal to find you. How did you manage to meet us at the gate? I thought only airplane passengers were allowed in this area."

"I received clearance from the airport security to be here to meet you." The warmth was back in his voice and expression as he smiled down at his oldest daughter.

Marsha had inherited her father's dark coloring and the dimple in his chin, while Annette appeared to have only Jordan Long's gray eyes. Yet Kathleen had the impression as she studied the rapport between the father and his oldest daughter that there was a great deal more of Jordan Long in Annette than in Marsha.

"How was your flight?" Annette asked, then rushed on before he had a chance to answer. "Ours was really bumpy, but Marsha didn't get sick once. Kathleen—she's a nurse, you know—she gave her some airsick pills when we got to the airport and sat with her all the way. Actually I think it's all in Marsha's mind, don't you?"

"I doubt if Marsha thinks so," Kathleen inserted with a gentle smile at Marsha's still wan face. Instantly she wished she had kept silent as the piercing steel gaze was again focused on her.

"What hotel are we staying at?" Again Annette distracted his attention. "Are we going to do anything tonight? Heavens!" she exclaimed, her gray eyes widening as she glanced at Kathleen. "We still have to pick up our luggage! If they lost our bags, I'll just die! We went shopping the other day and Kathleen helped me pick out this really super outfit. It's the latest fashion. I look terrific in it and I can hardly wait until you see me wearing it. You don't think they would have forgotten to unload our luggage from the plane, do you, dad?"

"We'll have to go to the baggage claim area to find out, I guess," he replied with indulging humor.

As they all turned down the corridor, Kathleen followed a step behind and to one side. The two girls flanked him, with Annette walking with her usual buoyancy on his left and the more reserved Marsha on his right.

"I got a new outfit, too," Marsha spoke up. The weakness in her voice betrayed the tranquilizing effect of the motion-sickness pill. "It's blue. Kathleen said it matched my eyes."

There were two truths in her statement. Marsha did have a new outfit and it was blue, but Kathleen couldn't remember making any comment about it matching her eyes.

"You never did say what we were going to do tonight, dad," Annette reminded him.

"Nothing," Jordan Long replied. "By the time we recover your luggage, drive from the airport to the hotel, check into our rooms and have dinner, it will be late enough for you girls to be in bed."

"The translation of that is you're suffering from jet lag and are too tired to take us anywhere," Annette teased.

"Right on the first guess," he chuckled.

Annette kept up a steady stream of chatter all the way to the baggage claim area while Kathleen unobtrusively studied her employer. Now that she had met him, she could well understand why the company found him so invaluable in the role of a troubleshooter.

There was the same bearing of total self-confidence that she had noted in Annette. He was intelligent, the type of man that could assess a situation and come to a quick decision. The aura of male vitality about him would command the respect of men and attract the admiration of women. Kathleen had been exposed briefly to his masculine charm in those few minutes before he had realized who she was. She knew its potency.

The abrupt change in his manner allowed her another glimpse of his character. Obviously he could deal quite ruthlessly with an adversary. She was still puzzling over the reason for the change and coming no nearer to a logical cause. She had the uneasy feeling that before the night was over she would find out why.

There was a large crowd milling about the baggage claim area when they arrived. As a nurse, Kathleen had learned to anticipate the needs of others, both doctors and patients. She had the claim tickets ready when Jordan Long requested them. His hard expression was icily aloof, a grimly forbidding line to his mouth.

All their luggage arrived safely. A porter wheeled it to an exit door and waited with Kathleen and the girls for Jordan to drive up in the sedan he had rented for the weekend. Annette immediately hopped into the front seat with her father while the porter stowed their luggage in the trunk with Jordan's. Her action relegated Kathleen and Marsha to the back seat.

Kathleen had thought her position behind the driver would isolate her, but she hadn't counted on the rear view mirror. It provided her with a clear view of the strongly etched features of Jordan Long and an equally unobstructed view for him of her. As he shifted the car into gear, their glances locked in the mirror. His was hard and challenging while Kathleen's was puzzled by his apparent animosity.

Try as she would, Kathleen couldn't keep her gaze from straying to the ruggedly handsome face in the mirror during the drive to their hotel. She paid little attention to the conversation flowing between Annette and her father. From the look of absent concentration on his face, she guessed that Jordan Long wasn't giving it his undivided attention either.

A sixth sense warned her that she was the object of his harsh contemplation. The sensation was reinforced the few times her gaze inadvertently was caught by his.

Jordan Long had reserved a suite of rooms at the hotel. Kathleen's small room was connected to the girls' by a shared bathroom. Theirs was separated from his by a small sitting room. The accommodation was faultless, but Kathleen didn't have much of an opportunity to dwell on it as she unpacked her clothes and helped the girls. She had a few minutes to freshen up before it was time to go down to the hotel restaurant for dinner.

4

The food had been delicious, but Kathleen thought she could have enjoyed it more if she had been less aware of the undercurrents of hostility coming from Jordan Long. The rare comments he directed at her had been issued with thinly disguised politeness.

Fortunately both of the girls had seemed oblivious to his chilling attitude toward her. Marsha had picked nervously at her food, leaving most of it on her plate, but Kathleen had not blamed it on the tension in the air. She doubted that the young girl had fully recovered from the flight. As for Annette, nothing seemed to shake her.

It had been something of a relief when Jordan had finished his coffee and suggested it was time they went up to their rooms. As it turned out, Kathleen's relief was short-lived.

When they entered the small sitting room, Jordan instructed, "You girls go into your room and get ready for bed. Miss Darrow and I are going to have a little talk." His gaze flicked to her with the sharpness of a whip.

"It's too early, dad," Annette said.

"It will be nearly ten by the time you change and crawl into bed, so off you go," he ordered in a tone that would not tolerate any arguments.

Grumbling beneath her breath, Annette sulked toward the door to the bedroom she shared with Marsha. Her younger sister seemed almost eager to leave. Kathleen wished she could join them when she cast a sideways glance through her lashes at the uncompromising hardness etched in Jordan Long's face.

At the click of the latch indicating that the door was tightly closed between the two rooms, he turned toward her, his gaze coldly sweeping over her. Kathleen kept her expression composed, although a bewildered light entered her eyes.

"Have a seat, Miss Darrow." The command was clipped out.

Kathleen obeyed. "What was it you wanted to discuss with me?" she inquired calmly.

He had remained standing, increasing the sensation that he was towering above her like an angry avenger. Having to look even higher up at him put her at a greater disadvantage, as she guessed he knew it would.

He didn't immediately respond to her question. Long, smooth strides took him to a small table sitting against the wall. A briefcase was on top of it. He removed a folder and separated a paper from the others. Walking back, he handed it to her.

"Would you please explain the meaning of this, Miss Darrow?" Jordan challenged coldly.

A muscle twitched in the strong jaw. Kathleen sensed that the anger that had been building since they met was now held in check by a very slim thread. Her gaze slowly withdrew from its study of his face to examine the paper he had thrust in her hand.

The writing on the form she recognized instantly as her own. She was even more bewildered when she looked at him again. "I don't understand." She frowned in confusion. "This is my application."

Fire smoldered in his charcoal eyes at her admission. "How old are you, Miss Darrow?" he accused.

Her frown deepened. "Twenty-five." Were they back to the age problem?

"What does your application say that your age is?" Jordan Long demanded tightly.

Kathleen glanced bewilderedly at the section of the form where her birth-date was. She looked at it once, blinked and looked at it again. It wasn't possible!

"I...I'm afraid there's been a mistake." An abrupt, self-conscious laugh accompanied her words.

"A very large mistake, I would say." The words of agreement were drawn out very slowly and very precisely.

"The numbers for the year I was born are inverted," she murmured, looking back at the application when she was unable to hold the rapier thrust of his piercing gaze.

"Were you aware of my requirements when you applied for the position, Miss Darrow?" The softness of his accusing voice filled her with dread.

Her tongue nervously touched a corner of her mouth.

"You are referring to the fact that you had wanted someone older, aren't you?" Considering the turmoil that was going on inside, her voice sounded very composed.

"Then you did know," Jordan Long returned with pinning hardness.

"Yes, I was aware of it—"She had been about to say that she had understood her qualifications had overridden the age factor, but he didn't give her the chance.

"Which is why you deliberately lied about your age."

"That's not true!" Kathleen protested sharply.

"Is that your handwriting?" he retorted sharply.

Her temper flared and she quickly counted to ten. "Yes, it is my handwriting," she admitted evenly, "but I assure you the date I have written here is simply an honest mistake. The numbers are right, but in the wrong order."

"A very pat and almost believable explanation." His mouth twisted into a mocking smile. "You knew I would find out eventually. What did you hope to gain by the deception? Enough time to settle into my home and get acquainted with my daughters, to show me how capable and reliable you are so that even when I knew the truth, I wouldn't be inclined to fire you."

"I did not do this deliberately!" Kathleen repeated forcefully. "I wasn't trying to deceive you just to get the job." Her hand waved through the air in a hopeless gesture toward the bedroom. "Mrs. Long and your daughters were aware of my age. If I had been trying to trick you, then why did I let them know?"

His expression didn't change as he ignored her question. "I imagine it was easy to charm an old lady and two young girls into recommending you. Since I was out of the country, there would only be their comments and your falsified application for me to review. It was a very clever plan, Miss Darrow."

The temperature in the room seemed to be rising steadily. Kathleen unbuttoned her ivory jacket and rose to her feet. She was beginning to get a crick in her neck from looking up at him all the time.

"I did not plan this," she insisted.

"Why were you so eager to have this particular job?" His gaze narrowed thoughtfully, black lashes veiling the dark smoke of his eyes.

"Because I thought I would like it and I do," Kathleen flashed in irritation. "There was no ulterior motive."

"Wasn't there?" Jordan Long mocked jeeringly. "You're a trained nurse, an excellent one if your references were true. There's no lack of openings for a good nurse."

"I wanted a change." She began breathing slowly to control her growing temper. "Nursing and hospitals were becoming my whole life, and that wasn't what I wanted. Besides, nurses are not that well paid."

"I see, then it was money. It must have sounded like a very cushy job, looking after two nearly grown girls, receiving room and board and a generous salary with an employer who was absent the better part of a year."

"I did not look at it that way at all," she replied tightly.

"Come now, Miss Darrow," he jeered, his head tilting to an arrogant angle. "If it wasn't the money, then what prompted you to take a job that promised so little free time and isolated you in the quiet countryside away from city life with only two young girls for company? Were you jilted by some man and decided to run away to nurse your broken heart?"

"I was not jilted, so I have no broken heart." Her voice trembled in anger. "If I'm doing any running then it's to a new way of life. I like the country and I like your daughters. And I don't particularly care whether you believe that or not!"

"And that's the only reason you lied about your age? You don't expect me to believe that."

"I did not lie about my age!" His steel gaze slashed pointedly to the application still in her hand. Kathleen thrust it onto the small table where the briefcase lay, as if the paper had scorched her fingers. "Not consciously I didn't," she qualified, since the evidence so obviously pointed to the opposite. "And I don't see why age is such a factor. I'm just as capable of taking care of your daughters and your home as an older woman who is twice my age. And I take my responsibilities seriously. I don't shirk them or consider my position as any sort of vacation."

"You can't be that naive, Miss Darrow." He towered beside her, the material of his jacket brushing the thin fabric of her blouse sleeve. His gaze held hers for a moment, then traveled slowly down the front of her blouse, dwelling on the agitated rise and fall of her breasts beneath the thin fabric. "Can't you think of one reason why it might not be suitable for a woman as young and attractive as you are to stay in my house?" Jordan Long spoke softly and suggestively.

No woman could possibly remain indifferent to the almost physical touch of his eyes. Kathleen was not an exception as hot flames licked her cheeks. She took a quick step away. A wicked glint of laughter danced in his eyes, and she hated herself for betraying her awareness of him.

"Were you hoping I would be a balding middle-aged man that you could twist around your finger?" he mocked. "Someone who would be taken in by your auburn hair and that flash of green in your eyes? Did you think to persuade him to accept you as an older daughter? Or were you going to appeal to his baser instincts?"

"You're disgusting!" Her temper exposed, Kathleen didn't try to regain control of it. "The only way I intended to 'please' my employer was to do my job well and conscientiously. I was hired—by you, Mr. Long—to look after your daughters and your home. Nothing else! You're my employer, and that is the only relationship we have or ever will have!"

"Really, Miss Darrow?" His composure wasn't disturbed by her burst of anger. "And that smile you gave me at the airport—it wasn't an invitation to get to know you better?"

"It was not!" she denied vehemently and turned away. It wasn't altogether the truth, since her reaction to his admiring look had been strictly feminine and not that of an employee meeting her boss for the first time.

"I must have read something more into it," Jordan Long replied in a voice that didn't believe her denial.

"You certainly did!"

"It doesn't really matter, because you won't be around long enough to find out which of us is right. My mistake in judgment was delegating the responsibility of interviewing applicants to someone else. It's a mistake I won't repeat. Fortunately I kept the other applications for the post—"

WITH HER EAR PRESSED against the connecting door, Annette listened intently to the conversation in the sitting room. She grimaced at her father's words and glanced at Marsha.

"He's going to fire her," she said in a moaning whisper. "We've got to do something."

"What?" Marsha's lower lip trembled. "He'll just get madder if he finds out what we've done."

Annette flashed her a speaking glance. "I don't think he can get much madder than he is right now, do you?"

"Poor Kathleen," Marsha murmured sympathetically. "I was really beginning to like her a lot."

"So was I," came Annette's whispered agreement. "There's just got to be something we can do to gain time."

"I'll just die if he hires the dragon lady."

A scheming light flashed in the gray smoke of Annette's eyes. "You won't die. You'll be sick!"

"What?" Marsha blinked her blue eyes.

"Come on. We haven't much time," Annette whispered urgently.

On tiptoe, she hurried as fast as she dared to the bathroom with her curious and confused younger sister mimicking her actions. Turning on the hot water tap in the sink, Annette slipped a washcloth under the running water.

"What are we doing?" Marsha persisted, frowning at her sister's action. "What did you mean when you said I'd be sick?"

"Just what I told you," she answered quietly. "You're going to pretend you're sick. It's the only thing I can think of to make them stop arguing, so at least I'll have time to think of something else," Annette explained. She wrung most of the water out of the washcloth. The mirror above the sink was steaming. "Hold this cloth on your face. It will make your skin feel hot as if you had a fever."

"It's hot!" Marsha protested, making a face as the cloth touched her skin.

"Do you want Kathleen to leave?" Annette's hands were on her hips.

"No," was the sigh, and the washcloth gingerly wrapped Marsha's cheeks and her forehead.

Annette waited for a few seconds to see the results. With a satisfied nod, she rinsed the washcloth again in hot water and handed it back.

"Now, hop into bed. All you have to do is be real weak. Every once in a while you can moan as if you don't feel very good. But don't overdo it," Annette cautioned in a fiercely low voice. "When I call them into the bedroom, you ask Kathleen to stay with you."

"Yes." Marsha bobbed her head as Annette led her to one of the twin beds in the room. "Why does it have to be me? Why can't you be sick?"

"Because—" Annette's patience was wearing thin "—I never am sick and you are." She rumpled the bedcovers as Marsha slid between the sheets, then mussed up her own bed and ruffled her short blond hair. "Are you ready?"

"I guess so," Marsha mumbled.

"Throw the washcloth under the bed." Annette started towards the connecting door. "Here goes emergency plan plus two!"

"YOU'RE PLANNING TO FIRE ME before you've even found out whether I'm capable or not," Kathleen stated angrily. "There's only one reason I can think of why you would be doing that. You're the one who doesn't trust himself to have me in the house. You're one of those pawing men who have to make a conquest of every woman they meet to prove to themselves that they're still men."

"Hardly, Miss Darrow." His lips curled contemptuously. "I don't like it when people try to take advantage of me or my family. Nor do I like it when people try to get things under false pretenses as you have done."

"I've told you repeatedly that the mistake on the application was an inadvertent one. I—"

"Kathleen!" Annette's voice called frantically from the connecting room, followed immediately by a knock on the door before it burst open. "Kathleen, it's Marsha. She's sick. Will you come?"

Kathleen was already reacting to the alarm in Annette's voice and was halfway to the door before Annette gave the explanation for her interruption. She was vaguely aware of Jordan Long following her as she hurried into the adjoining room.

Marsha was lying in the far twin bed with her eyes closed. She opened them as Kathleen bent over her. The blue eyes were wide and slightly frightened, and Kathleen smiled reassuringly.

"What's the matter, Marsha?" she asked gently, placing a hand against the girl's flushed cheeks.

"I don't feel good," came the murmured reply.

The hesitant blue eyes swung past Kathleen, then the lashes fluttered weakly down. The hands gripping the covers trembled slightly. Kathleen glanced sideways, her gaze catching the broad chest of Jordan Long and rising quickly to his face. Simultaneously, his gray eyes flicked from the face of his daughter to her.

The anger of a moment ago was forgotten. Kathleen easily slipped into her previous professional role, responding to the concern in his face.

"She seems to have a slight fever." She answered the unspoken question in his gaze. Her attention reverted to Marsha. "Is your stomach upset, Marsha?"

The lashes opened to reveal rounded eyes and Marsha moved her head in a small affirmative nod.

Annette moved around to the opposite side of the bed. "I suppose it's the aftereffect of the plane ride, don't you, Kathleen?" she suggested. "I mean, she gets so nervous and all."

"I don't think it's anything serious," Kathleen agreed, offering Marsha another gentle smile of commiseration, "Have you thrown up?"

"No," she answered weakly, then moaned softly as Annette sat on the bed beside her. "But I kinda feel like I might."

"You just lie there and be quiet for a while. Breathe slowly." Kathleen took hold of her wrist and checked her pulse. With a glance at Jordan, she said softly, "It's normal."

"Will—will you stay with me, Kathleen?" The blue eyes gazed at her imploringly.

"Of course I will," she agreed. She glanced around the room, her gaze settling on a chair in the corner. "I'll sit right here beside you until you go to sleep. How's that?"

"Fine." A tiny smile curved Marsha's mouth.

While Kathleen moved away from the bed to fetch the chair, Jordan Long stepped closer to his daughter. He leaned over and lightly kissed her forehead.

"Everything will be all right, honey," he murmured and smiled, deepening the cleft in his strong chin.

He turned as Kathleen came back carrying the chair. Taking it from her, he set it next to his daughter's bed. When she started to walk past him, he moved slightly to block her way for an instant.

"We'll finish our discussion in the morning," he said quietly.

Her chin raised a fraction of an inch. "Of course, Mr. Long," Kathleen agreed curtly.

There was really very little left to discuss. He had made it abundantly plain that he was going to fire her. Obviously he had a few more jeering remarks he wanted to make. As he walked from the room, she sat down in the chair, taking the hand that Marsha held out to her and holding it lightly in her own.

With the excitement over, Annette returned to her own bed and crawled beneath the covers. "I'm glad you were here, Kathleen," she said simply. "Marsha gets a little frightened when she doesn't feel good."

"So does everyone," Kathleen smiled. "Good night, Annette."

"Good night."

"And you try to sleep," Kathleen told Marsha in a voice that was genuinely loving in its scolding tones.

"I will," Marsha agreed obediently. "Thank you for staying with me."

"You don't need to thank me." She shook her head slightly. "Good night."

"Good night." And Marsha closed her eyes.

It was nearly an hour before Kathleen was satisfied that Marsha was sleeping soundly, although still clutching Kathleen's hand. Gently she pried her hand free and tucked the covers around the sleeping girl before quietly returning to her own room. She left the door slightly ajar so she could hear Marsha if she called for her in the night.

VERY QUIETLY, Annette pushed back the covers and reached for her watch on the night table between the two beds. The luminous dial revealed that the time was two-thirty in the morning. She slipped from her bed and walked silently to her sister's.

"Marsha!" She shook the girl's shoulder until she got a response.

"Wh—"

"Ssh!" Annette held a silencing finger to her mouth. Tiptoeing to the door Kathleen had left open, she closed it very carefully, then tiptoed back to the bed. "You're going to have to be sick again," she whispered.

41

"Why?" Marsha frowned sleepily.

"Because you heard dad last night. He said they'd finish their talk in the morning, and we're going to have to convince Kathleen that you're still sick. We have to keep them apart for a while longer."

"What do I have to do this time?" Marsha yawned and rubbed her eyes as she pushed herself into a sitting position.

"Come on. We're going into the bathroom," Annette instructed.

Reluctantly Marsha climbed out of bed and followed her older sister. "It hardly seems fair to trick Kathleen this way," she mumbled.

"If we don't, then she'll leave and we'll never see her again," Annette pointed out. "Now you sit down there by the toilet and look sick."

Scurrying like a silent mouse, Annette hurried to open the connecting door to Kathleen's room, leaving it partially ajar the way it had been.

KATHLEEN STIRRED beneath the covers, her subconscious prodding her to waken. At the urgent call of her name, she was instantly awake, flinging back the covers and slipping out of bed. Static electricity molded her nightgown to her figure.

"Kathleen!" Annette was in the doorway. "Marsha's in the bathroom."

With Annette leading the way, Kathleen hurried into the bathroom. Marsha was sitting on the floor and leaning against the bathroom wall. She looked exhausted and weak as she glanced up.

"I'm sorry, Kathleen," she murmured.

"You don't have to be sorry," Kathleen soothed. "You couldn't help it."

She knelt beside her, noting the slight pallor in the cheeks that were cool to the touch of her hand. Marsha's respiration seemed even, although there was a faint skip to her pulse.

"Would you like to go back to bed now?" Kathleen asked.

There was a wide-eyed nod of agreement. Annette stepped forward as a door opened and footsteps approached. Kathleen turned slightly.

"Maybe we should help her," Annette suggested. "She seems awfully weak."

"Yes—"

Jordan Long stood in the doorway, his gray eyes sweeping over them in quick assessment. He was wearing only a pair of dark slacks. His ebony dark hair was tousled from sleep, springing in a disordered way that was oddly attractive. Inadvertently, Kathleen's gaze was drawn to the naked expanse of his suntanned and muscular chest. Then it was her pulse that suddenly began behaving erratically.

"Marsha was sick again," she explained unnecessarily, averting her gaze and keeping the mask of composure on her face. "We were just about to help her back to bed."

"I'll do it." He stepped into the small room, seeming to fill it with the force of his presence. His hard shoulder brushed her arm as he moved toward his youngest daughter, searing her skin with its warmth.

When he had gathered Marsha in his arms, Kathleen moved swiftly into the girls' room and pulled back the covers on Marsha's bed. With Marsha in bed, Kathleen sat on the edge, tucking the covers around the girl.

"Are you having any pains in your stomach, Marsha?" she asked.

There was a negative shake of the dark head on the pillow. "It just doesn't feel good," was the answer.

Glancing up at Jordan Long standing beside the bed, Kathleen queried, "Has she had any appendix trouble?"

"It's already been removed—when she was eight," he answered briskly, eliminating that possible explanation. The steel gaze raked harshly over Kathleen. "Miss Darrow, I think my daughter will survive long enough for you to go and put a robe on."

Her head jerked back with a start, a hand instinctively moving to the gaping neckline of her nightgown.

Pink dots appeared on her cheekbones while a resentful sparkle of green flashed in her hazel eyes. She refused to be hurried by the sarcastic censure in his low voice and turned instead to Marsha.

"I'll be right back," she promised, and returned suitably robed a few minutes later. Jordan Long departed immediately.

The next morning Marsha claimed to be no better. There weren't enough physical indications for Kathleen to feel the girl warranted the attention of a doctor. She couldn't believe it was still a nervous reaction to the plane ride and said as much.

"Maybe," Annette said hesitantly, glancing at her father who was standing in the far corner of the girls' room, "she's worrying about the fact that she has to get back on the plane the day after tomorrow."

"Is that what's bothering you?" Kathleen tipped her auburn head inquiringly.

There was a sliding glance at Annette before Marsha nodded silently that it was. Inwardly Kathleen sighed. It was so difficult to tell a child not to worry about something that seemed terrifying.

"Dad, I've been thinking," Annette said. "Maybe we should go back to Delaware I mean, it was a great idea you had for us to see Washington, but— well, let's face it, Marsha has really put a damper on the trip. We can come another time by car, can't we?"

"I think that, under the circumstances—"his gaze narrowed briefly on Kathleen"—you're right. None of us is in the mood for sight-seeing. I'll change the booking of our return flight to today."

"I'll pack your clothes, Marsha." Annette was already walking toward the closet.

"It will all be over in a little while, Marsha," Jordan Long said, moving toward the door.

Prophetic words, Kathleen thought, since once they had returned, it would all be over for her. She imagined that Jordan Long would have her packing her belongings and leaving before the day was over.

In these two short weeks, she had become rather fond of Marsha and Annette. The charges against her were false, but there was very little she could do to prove it. Even if she could, considering the harshness of the exchange with her employer, she didn't think it was wise to try.

5

The two girls were already at the door when Jordan Long laid a hand on Kathleen's arm, sunbrowned fingers contrasting sharply against the golden tint of her skin.

"Don't bother to unpack your things, Miss Darrow," he murmured as she glanced up to meet wintry gray eyes.

"I didn't intend to," she replied coolly, knowing very well what he meant by that remark and determined not to give him the chance to assail her with more of his insults while he fired her. "I cleaned the house thoroughly before we left and there's plenty of food in the kitchen. I'm sure you and the girls can prepare your own meal tonight."

His mouth thinned into a grim line. "If you'll step into my study, I'll write you out a check for the time you've worked."

Unbidden, the lines from a nursery rhyme sprang into her mind. "Will you step into my parlor, said the spider to the fly." Kathleen felt decidedly like the fly, only more wary.

Ignored by the adults conversing in low tones in the entry hall, Annette and Marsha paused on the first steps of the stairs. Annette was nibbling again on her lower lip, her expression one of deep concentration.

"What are we going to do?" Marsha whispered. Grimacing slightly, she added, "Do I have to be sick again?"

"We'd never get away with a third time." Annette's opinion of the question was evidenced by the impatient frown she gave her sister. "No, we're going to have to be straightforward this time. You just follow my lead and agree with whatever I say, okay?"

KATHLEEN REMAINED standing while Jordan Long walked around the walnut desk to sit in the swivel rocker. Her mind flashed back to the day when Annette had sat there and begun the interview. Now the girl's father was terminating the job with his signature on a check.

What she would have liked to do was tear the check up and throw it in his face, but starting a scene would be pointless. It would accomplish nothing but to arouse his anger. No, she would accept the check with all the dignity she possessed. Despite what he thought of her, she had earned it.

There was a knock at the study door before it swung open. Annette strolled nonchalantly into the room with Marsha shadowing her. Without a word, Annette sat at one end of the small sofa and Marsha at the other.

"I thought you girls had gone upstairs to unpack," Jordan Long stated crisply, his hand poised above the checkbook.

"We decided to do it later," Annette shrugged, plucking aimlessly at the cord edging of the sofa's arm.

"Would you mind leaving the room? Miss Darrow and I are having a private discussion." His gaze flicked briefly to Kathleen, then back to Annette.

"Actually—" Annette's tongue darted out to lick a corner of her mouth as she glanced from Kathleen to meet his commanding look "—it seems to me that what you're discussing is family business. Since Marsha and I are part of the family, we should take part in it, too. What is it that you're talking about?"

There was a tightening of his jaw as Jordan swerved his attention to the checkbook on the desk. He didn't reply immediately, pausing as though he was choosing his words with care. Kathleen remained silent. She wasn't about to explain to the girls the nature of her meeting with their father.

"I've decided that Miss Darrow isn't a suitable person to be looking after you girls," he said finally.

"Why?" Annette asked calmly.

"We like her," Marsha inserted.

"She's too young," was his reply.

"But you knew how old she was when you hired her," Annette pointed out, her eyes widening in blinking confusion.

46

"No, I wasn't aware of her age." Jordan Long shot Kathleen a look, plainly designed to remind her of the application. She smoldered inside but revealed none of her irritation. "I was under the impression she was older."

"You could have asked us." Annette glanced at her sister. "Marsha and I knew how old she was. So did Aunt Helen. Besides, we liked her better than the others who applied for the job—and now that we've got to know her, we like her even more."

"I'm sorry," he clipped the apology out. "But she's too young."

"What has age got to do with it?" Annette frowned. "With Kathleen it's like having an older sister to take care of us. You know how Aunt Helen was, and Miss Carmichael before that was a regular tyrant. And Mrs. Howard was so absentminded she'd forget where we were. Why can't Kathleen stay?"

His patience was thinning at an alarming rate. "Annette, you're old enough to realize a few facts about life. It wouldn't be proper for a young woman such as Miss Darrow to be living in this house."

Annette looked at him blankly for a moment before a light dawned in her eyes. "Oh, I get it!" she exclaimed. "You think that other people might think you and Kathleen are having an affair. Really, that's ridiculous, daddy!" she laughed.

"Is it?" A black eyebrow arched arrogantly at his daughter's open amusement.

"Of course it is," Annette insisted with the wide grin still splitting her face. "You're much too old for Kathleen ever to be interested in you that way. Good grief, dad, you're thirty-seven years old!" she exclaimed, as if he was approaching antiquity instead of being a man in his prime. "You're practically old enough to be her father!"

Kathleen pressed her lips tightly together to conceal the smile teasing the corners of her mouth. Covertly, she glanced at Jordan through her lashes. He didn't look very pleased with his daughter's assessment.

Annette wasn't finished. "And Kathleen isn't at all like the women you usually date. You like the blond, sophisticated type. And Kathleen is, well—" she seemed at a loss to find the words to describe her "—Kathleen is nice," she concluded lamely. Pricking Kathleen's ego, she hastened on with, "She's very pretty in her own way, but she just isn't the type of woman that you go for, dad."

Sardonic gray eyes glittered with amusement at Kathleen's expense as she was cut down to size as he had been a moment ago. Kathleen guessed that what Annette said was true. She could easily visualize Jordan Long with some cool, Nordic blonde on his arm.

"Besides, dad," Annette continued, "nobody who sees you would ever for one instant think of you as a dirty old man who's always chasing young girls. Not only that, Kathleen already has a boyfriend."

"Is that true?" A disbelieving look mocked Kathleen.

47

No doubt he still believed she was running away from a broken affair. For once in her life, Kathleen was very glad to claim Barry as her boyfriend and puncture Jordan Long's theory.

"Yes, it is true," she answered distinctly.

With a blink of his eye, he dismissed it as unimportant. "Your arguments are very clever, Annette, but they don't change my opinion that we should have someone older and more experienced."

"But what about our opinion?" Annette protested. "Don't we have some say in the matter? After all, Marsha and I are the ones most directly involved."

"Yes, and we want her to stay," Marsha chimed in.

"I appreciate the way you girls feel, but…" He began patiently but firmly to refuse their request.

"But you don't understand, dad," Annette interrupted. "We know you're only doing what you think is best for us, but look at it from our point of view. You're hardly ever home. I know you can't help it and that it's your job," she conceded. "Marsha and I understand that. Since you have to be away so much, we just want to stay with someone we like. And that someone is Kathleen. You can't argue that she isn't qualified for the job, because you know she is."

"We would still miss you as much as ever, dad," Marsha added earnestly. "But we wouldn't be quite so lonely if Kathleen lived here with us."

Kathleen could see by the grim expression on his ruggedly handsome features that the girls had backed him into a corner. As much as she liked the job, she didn't want to keep it simply because he had been pressured into reversing his decision.

"Listen," she spoke up hesitantly, glancing at the girls in turn. "I appreciate your support and the fact that you like me well enough to want me to stay, but I really think it might be best if I didn't stay. Because of a misunderstanding, your father and I have got off on the wrong foot."

"But he'll like you as much as we do, once he gets to know you," Annette insisted.

"Please, don't go," Marsha begged openly. "No one else has ever cared about us as much as you do. If daddy says you can stay, please promise that you will."

Tears welled in the pleading blue eyes, one spilling out at the corner and trickling down Marsha's cheek. A person would have to be made of stone to resist that appeal, and Kathleen was not.

"Oh, Marsha!" she sighed, smiling tightly and helplessly looking at Jordan Long.

The tearful gaze switched to him as well. "Please, daddy, say that Kathleen can stay."

Breathing in deeply, he stared at the checkbook on the desktop, then flipped it shut. "A month's trial period," he conceded grudgingly, sending a

48

piercing look at his daughter. "If, at the end of a month, I decide that Miss Darrow isn't suitable, I don't want to hear any more about it from you girls. Is that agreed?"

"Thank you, daddy!" Marsha burst out, her face wreathed in a smile as she nodded agreement.

"You won't be sorry," Annette added.

"I hope not," he muttered, his wintry look sliding to Kathleen. "Will you agree to a month's trial?"

"I seem to have as little choice in the matter as you do," she answered, since they had both been victims of the emotional blackmail of the girls. "Yes, I agree to it," she replied, although she doubted that she would be retained after the month came to an end.

"Come on, Marsha. Let's go and unpack for Kathleen," Annette suggested in a triumphant voice, and the two girls raced happily from the study.

But Kathleen was not yet dismissed. "I hope you understand, Miss Darrow, that when I suggested this month's trial, I was not condoning the trickery you used to obtain the position in the first place."

Kathleen swallowed back the retort that she had not set out deliberately to trick him. He wouldn't believe her anyway.

"It never occurred to me that you were," she replied.

"I have a week's leave coming and another week of work before my vacation begins," Jordan Long continued.

"That should work out quite well, then," Kathleen interrupted. "You'll have ample time to find an older and more qualified replacement for me—and without having to rely on pieces of paper," she said, letting him know that she was aware the month's trial was a farcical agreement perpetrated for the benefit of the girls.

A humorless smile of cynicism curved his mouth.

"I'm glad we understand each other."

"Perfectly, Mr. Long." When she turned to leave, he didn't stop her.

"WHAT A PERFORMANCE!" Annette exclaimed, throwing her arms in the air and spinning around Kathleen's bedroom. "Oh, Marsha, you were super! Those tears were just the thing. I never knew you were such a good actress! 'I would miss you, daddy, but I wouldn't be so lonely if Kathleen was with us,'" she said, mimicking her sister's plea and giggling.

Marsha self-consciously wiped away the wet trail on her cheek. "I wasn't acting. I meant every word I said," she replied stiffly.

Annette tipped her head to one side, the gleeful amusement gone from her expression as she regarded her sister with wide-eyed wonder.

"You really do like Kathleen that much, don't you?" she said.

49

"Yes," Marsha mumbled, watching her hand trailing over the suitcase on the bed.

"Well—" Annette shrugged "—that's all the more reason why we have to be sure that she stays."

"Daddy is so angry about that application. He hates it when people lie," came the sighing words of defeat.

"He'll get over it," Annette answered confidently. "We'll see to that and so will Kathleen."

"I hope you're right," Marsha murmured doubtfully.

"I know I am."

THE CHILLING TRUCE that followed put Kathleen on her mettle. Although the month's outcome would be the same regardless, Jordan Long was not going to be able to fault her work.

As she and the girls cleared the Monday evening dishes, she noticed with satisfaction the way he had thoroughly cleaned his plate. It was a compliment to her cooking skill, whether he wanted to admit it or not.

The telephone rang in the living room. Since his return, there had been a surfeit of telephone calls. Kathleen ignored the ring, aware that he was in the living room and the call was undoubtedly for him anyway. It was something of a surprise when she picked up the tray of dishes and saw him standing in the dining room.

"The phone call is for you, Miss Darrow. I believe it's your boyfriend," he added dryly.

"I'll take the tray." Annette appeared at her side. "Marsha and I will take care of the dishes. You go and talk to Barry."

"Thank you." Kathleen handed the tray to her, wondering why she suddenly felt so self-conscious. She was, after all, entitled to receive personal phone calls.

As she walked unhurriedly into the living room, she was aware that Jordan followed at a leisurely pace. He paused at one of the windows to gaze at the purpling dusk. Warily, Kathleen glanced at him, tucking her auburn hair behind her ear as she picked up the phone. His expression was one of absent concentration, seemingly oblivious to her presence. She wished she could say the same.

"Hello." She turned her back to him, hoping that by removing the strong profile from her vision she could ignore him.

"Hello, Kathleen." Barry's voice returned her greeting with considerably more enthusiasm. "Was that your Mr. Long who answered the phone?"

Your Mr. Long—a poor choice of words, she thought silently. "Yes," she admitted. It was impossible to correct his wording, not when Jordan could overhear her.

"Was he anything like you expected?" he asked curiously.

She hadn't gone so far as forming an image in her mind of what Jordan Long would look like, but she doubted if she would ever have visualized the tall, vitally attractive man in the living room with her now.

"No, I guess not."

A low chuckle sounded over the receiver. "I take it by your noncommittal replies that he's in the room with you."

"That's right." Kathleen laughed softly at her carefully worded answers, designed not to let Jordan Long guess that he was under discussion.

"How was your trip to Washington, D.C., then?"

"It ended almost before it began," she explained. "Marsha got sick and we came home on Saturday morning."

"Nothing serious, I hope." There was instant concern in his voice.

"A case of nerves, I think. She's afraid of flying, and I guess that upset her. She was fine after we came home." Kathleen was unaware of using the word home. Subconsciously it was the way she thought of the Long house.

"I was going to suggest that I come out to see you tonight, but I suppose you won't think I should, with your boss being there and all," he sighed.

"No, I don't think it would be a good idea," she agreed, "not tonight, anyway."

"Miss Darrow," Jordan Long's voice interrupted briskly, causing Kathleen to pivot sharply toward him.

"Excuse me a minute, Barry," she said into the telephone, then covered the receiver with her hand. "Did you want something, Mr. Long?"

"I'll be taking the girls with me to Dover on Thursday. You're free to make whatever plans you wish for that day," he informed her, obviously assuming that she would want to spend the time with Barry. Kathleen held his steady gray look for several seconds as she removed her hand from the receiver. "Barry? Mr. Long has just told me that I'll have Thursday off this week. Will you be free for lunch that day?"

There was a glitter of contempt in Jordan's gaze as it raked her curved figure before he turned away. She guessed that he disapproved of women who did the asking. He was undoubtedly the type that liked to do all the chasing, even when he knew the object of his attention wanted to be caught. And she couldn't imagine any woman, with the possible exclusion of herself, who wouldn't want to be caught by him.

"Yes, I'll be free on Thursday," Barry replied.

"I'll meet you at twelve-thirty at your office," Kathleen suggested.

"Make it eleven-thirty instead," he replied. "Then you can tell me all about your employer," he added.

"Yes, yes, of course," she acknowledged haltingly, unsure at this point of how much she wanted to tell. "I'll see you on Thursday."

There was no other comment from Jordan Long when Kathleen hung up the receiver. In fact he didn't even glance her way as she left the living room for the kitchen, but continued staring out the window in a preoccupied fashion.

On Thursday morning, rain drizzled from the gloomy, cloud-covered sky. It was hardly the type of day that encouraged a person to go out, Kathleen sighed to herself. She sipped at her coffee, but not even the fragrant aroma seemed able to perk up her spirits.

Annette drained her orange juice glass and sat back in her chair at the breakfast table. Marsha was still eating her bowl of cereal, and Jordan was hidden behind the morning newspaper opposite Kathleen.

"Why don't you drive into Dover with us, Kathleen?" Annette suggested. "Aunt Helen said she invited you to come with us the other day when you talked to her. She did, didn't she?"

"Yes—"

The newspaper rustled as Jordan folded it down to gaze curiously at Kathleen. "You talked to Mrs. Long recently?" he questioned with an arrogant arch of his eyebrow.

"On Tuesday," she admitted.

"Kathleen calls her or has one of us call her every other day," Annette explained. "Just to make sure Aunt Helen is all right and to keep her from being lonely or thinking that we might not care about her any more."

"Very commendable, Miss Darrow."

But the glittering charcoal eyes emitted an entirely different message. Kathleen guessed that he thought she was doing it simply to impress him. She wasn't in the mood to convince him otherwise.

"Tell Mrs. Long when you see her that I've made other plans for today. Maybe I can call in another time." She addressed her reply to Annette.

"You're welcome to come with us, Miss Darrow. I can drop you off in town if you like." The paper was once more erected between them. It was a subtle and unnecessary reminder that he didn't particularly care whether she accepted or not.

"No, thank you," she refused. "I have some other personal errands to take care of and I wouldn't want to take you out of your way. Besides, I have my own car."

"It wouldn't be any trouble," Annette protested. "Tell her, daddy, that you don't mind."

"This is Miss Darrow's day off, Annette," Jordan reminded his daughter from behind his paper barricade. "She would probably like to spend it away from you girls."

"Must you keep calling her Miss Darrow?" Annette shook her head hopelessly at him. "It sounds so cold and unfriendly."

"I beg your pardon." The paper was folded up and placed on the table. Mocking gray eyes were focused on the auburn-haired girl across the table from him. "I didn't intend to sound unfriendly."

"It doesn't matter," Kathleen answered tightly, picking up her cup and drinking the remaining liquid. Annette was overly optimistic in thinking that her father would ever be friendly toward her, and Kathleen knew it.

"Is it true that you want to get away from Marsha and me?" The blond head was tipped curiously toward her.

"Not exactly," Kathleen denied.

"The fact is, Annette," Jordan inserted, "that Kathleen has a date with her boyfriend today. She wouldn't want you two girls as chaperones."

He used her given name so casually that for an instant Kathleen didn't realize he had said it. It sounded very different spoken by that low-pitched masculine voice.

Annette took the news quite blandly, accepting the explanation. "I hope we get to meet Barry some time. He sounds quite nice."

"Have you finished yet, Marsha?" Jordan glanced at his youngest daughter. "I'd like to leave before lunchtime," he teased lightly.

Marsha scooped out the last spoonful of cereal and announced that she was finished. As the three rose from the table, Jordan paused to look at the still seated Kathleen.

"You can leave the breakfast dishes, Kathleen." This time there was a sardonic emphasis on her name. "The girls will do them when we come back tonight." Without waiting for her reply, he turned away.

A few minutes later, the girls were calling their goodbyes as they slipped out through the side door into the closed garage.

There was plenty of time for her to do the dishes before she had to leave to meet Barry. Kathleen was inclined to do them, except that she knew Jordan Long would think she had washed them to make points with him. So instead she stacked them neatly on the counter beside the sink.

As she walked into the living room, laughter bubbled in her throat. She wondered what his reaction would be if she started calling him Jordan. She doubted that he would interpret it as a gesture of friendship. If anything, he would probably assume she was attempting some kind of feminine flirtation to persuade him to change his mind about her.

Kathleen was suddenly reminded of the way Jordan had looked at her at the airport, and a warmth seeped through her limbs at the picture in her mind. She wondered curiously what their relationship might have been if there hadn't been that embarrassing mix-up about her age. It was a very disturbing thought.

The telephone rang as she walked past it, and she jumped at its strident ring. Chiding herself for being foolish, she came out of her momentary daydream to answer it. It was Barry.

"Sorry, but I'm going to have to break our lunch date. It's a business commitment. I'll be lunching with a client," he explained quickly, as if Kathleen needed to be reassured he wasn't breaking a date with her to keep one with another girl.

"That's all right," she insisted, smiling at his almost painful earnestness. "I understand." Her gaze slid to the window and the rain misting the glass. "The weather is really dreadful today, and I wasn't all that eager to find a parking place close to your office," she laughed, since it was a near impossibility.

"I—I have a committee meeting tonight or I'd suggest that we have dinner instead of lunch together. I don't suppose there's any chance you'd be free Friday or Saturday night?"

"No." But Kathleen assured him again that she understood about his previous commitments. Secretly she discovered she was rather glad. It seemed she spent all her time bolstering his confidence, and at the moment she needed someone to reinforce her own.

They talked for several more minutes until Barry received a phone call on another line and had to hang up. Kathleen took a deep breath and glanced out the window. She had an entire day off with nothing to do.

There were no errands to run. She had made that up for Annette's benefit and to avoid being pressured into accepting Jordan's offer of a lift that she knew he didn't want to make. There was some shopping she could have done for personal items, but that could be accomplished when she did the household purchasing.

As she walked toward the staircase, Kathleen contemplated visiting her parents, but it was her mother's day for her church committee, so that was out. Maggie, Darla and Betty were working the day shift at the hospital, so she couldn't visit them. And the drizzling gray weather negated any outdoor activity. She certainly couldn't visit Helen Long, not with the girls and Jordan Long there.

In her room, Kathleen changed out of her bright yellow trouser suit, worn to make up for the lack of sunshine. Donning her old standby favorite of faded denims and bulky gray sweat shirt, she picked up the book on the bedside table and retraced her steps downstairs.

There was no point in going out, since there was nowhere to go. It was her free day to spend as she chose, she reminded herself. If she chose to spend it alone in the house, reading a book, surely it was nobody's business but her own.

Curling up on the sofa in the living room, Kathleen opened the book, but the gloomy weather outside seemed to press into the room, melancholy and depressing. She built a small fire in the fireplace, hoping the cozy sound of crackling flames would chase away the dreary atmosphere.

For a while the fire helped as she became immersed in the book she had read many times before. She began identifying with the heroine, Jane Eyre, until she realized it was Jordan Long she was picturing as her Rochester, and she closed the book with a snap. That would simply not do!

Rising, she began to pace the room restlessly. Forced idleness was not something she enjoyed. Mentally thumbing her nose at Jordan, she walked into the kitchen and washed up the breakfast dishes. He could think what he liked about why she had done them.

As she was putting the dishes away, a germ of an idea formed. The kitchen cupboards were in need of cleaning. New shelf paper was in the pantry. Kathleen had bought it last week with the intention of having Viola Kent, the cleaning woman, do them on Tuesday.

The whole day was before her—it was barely ten o'clock. She could easily clean all the cupboards and put down fresh paper before the Longs returned, and Jordan would never be the wiser. If he didn't know it, he couldn't possibly accuse her of doing it to impress him.

Considering his cynical attitude toward her, he would never understand the satisfaction she derived from cleaning. To Kathleen, the end results were ample reward for the work put in to make it that way. She didn't object to a certain amount of disorder. But luckily she hadn't gone over the edge and become a demon for cleanliness.

With the decision made, she set to work, flipping on the radio to fill the room with music and chase away the gloomy clouds pressing at the windows. Slipping out of her shoes, she set them out of the way under the breakfast table. It was a quirk of hers. She liked to be barefoot whenever she did any cleaning.

Starting with the cupboards containing the canned and packaged foodstuffs, she unloaded the shelves, removed the old paper and began wiping them out with a damp sponge.

6

The last cupboards were the most difficult because they were located above the refrigerator. Standing on a chair in front of the refrigerator, Kathleen hadn't been able to reach the top shelf nor the back of the lower shelf, so she had opted for a somewhat precarious perch, using the chair and the adjoining counter top to reach the shelves.

A matching set of glasses, goblets and punch bowl were stored on the two shelves. All of them were dusty from long disuse, and Kathleen washed them before returning them to the former place. Only the goblets remained to be put back.

With a knee on the counter and a barefoot waving in the air for balance, she stretched across the refrigerator top to set one goblet on the shelf. The radio was blaring in her ear.

"What are you doing?" a voice barked loudly from the direction of the side door into the garage.

Startled, Kathleen spun around. Her elbow hit the edge of an open cupboard door, sending needles of pain down her arm, momentarily paralyzing her fingers. The goblet tumbled from her hand, striking first the counter top, then breaking on the chair seat and shattering glass onto the tile floor.

"Don't move!" Jordan Long called out.

But the warning came too late. Instinct had already made Kathleen react quickly to try to catch the expensive crystal goblet before it broke. The sole of her bare foot came down on a piece of glass on the chair top. A stifled gasp of pain followed the piercing contact.

Not daring to move from the safety of her perch atop the counter, she sat down on the formica top, twisting her leg to view the injury to the bottom of her foot. There was a telltale smear of red and a stabbing pain.

"I thought I told you not to move!" Glass crunched under his shoes as Jordan strode angrily to her side.

Kathleen glanced at the masculine features, etched with impatience at her foolishness. "You did."

"What happened?" Annette appeared in the doorway to the garage, her gray eyes rounded with curiosity. Marsha was right behind her.

"Kathleen broke a goblet," Jordan answered abruptly. "Get a broom from the closet and sweep it up before someone else gets cut." He diverted his attention back to Kathleen, more specifically to her injured foot. "Let's see how bad it is," he ordered grimly.

"I am a nurse," she reminded him curtly as he pushed her probing fingers out of the way. "I'm certainly qualified to deal with a simple cut."

Steel gray eyes briefly met the stubborn flash of her gaze. "I've had some first aid experience and, unless you're a contortionist, I can see better than you whether there are any glass splinters in the wound."

Kathleen surrendered her foot grudgingly. "What are you doing back so early anyway?" she muttered, then winced involuntarily when he plucked out a glass chip.

"Four o'clock isn't exactly early." With the glass removed, the blood flowed more freely from the cut.

Deftly he wrapped his white handkerchief around her foot. Kathleen was still trying to register the fact that it was much later than she had thought when he slid an arm under her knees and another around her waist and back.

"What are you doing?" she protested in shock as he lifted her from the counter and cradled her against his chest.

Instinctively her hands wrapped themselves around his neck, as if afraid that at any moment he would drop her. But he seemed to find her weight no burden. The two girls were watching with wide-eyed looks.

At close quarters, the glitter of his eyes over her stunned face was disturbing. "I was going to carry you into the other room, unless you wanted to walk in your bare feet over some more glass," Jordan replied mockingly.

Pressing her lips together, Kathleen refused to comment on his remark and averted her gaze to the rolled collar of his white turtleneck. Her side vision saw the twitching of his mouth in an ill-concealed smile.

57

"Be sure to get all that glass cleaned up," he reminded the girls before he carried Kathleen through the door into the dining room. "Would you mind explaining to me what you were doing?"

"I wasn't stealing the crystal, if that's what you were thinking," she retorted. He didn't stop in the dining room but continued to the living room. "I was cleaning the cupboards. I was in the process of putting the goblets back when you shouted at me."

"Cleaning cupboards on your day off? My, but you're conscientious!" There was an underlying tone of ridicule in his voice.

"There was nothing else to do," Kathleen snapped in her own defense.

In the entry hall, she realized Jordan was carrying her to the master bedroom. It was on the tip of her tongue to remind him that the downstairs bathroom was much closer than the private one off his room. Then she decided to say nothing that would earn her any more of his gibes about conscience. After all, she had been in his bedroom any number of times, although never when he was there.

"Nothing else to do?" Jordan repeated her phrase. His dark head was tilted curiously down towards her. "What happened to the luncheon date with your boyfriend?"

"Cancelled. He had to meet a client."

Her senses were beginning to take notice of the steady beat of his heart and the intoxicating fragrance of after-shave lotion on his smooth cheeks. She could feel the rippling muscles in the arms that carried her. She didn't like being suddenly reminded of his striking masculinity just as he was about to sit her on his bed.

"Wait here," he ordered when she was seated on the beige coverlet, and walked into the adjoining bathroom.

Rather than submit to the decidedly intimate aura of the manly room, Kathleen crooked her leg to rest her injured foot on her other knee, removing his handkerchief bandage to investigate the wound. Jordan was back in seconds with disinfectant and bandages.

"Won't you be meeting—what was his name, Barry—this evening?" he questioned as he knelt on the floor beside her.

"No, Barry has a committee meeting tonight," she replied, straightening slightly to watch the competent sunbrowned hands clean the cut.

He smiled crookedly. "So you decided to vent your frustrations by cleaning the cupboards. My mother used to say that cleaning was the best way to get rid of anger."

"Really?" Kathleen tilted her head curiously to one side. "I just can't stand being idle. When I lose my temper, I count to ten and then throw something."

"Remind me to stay out of your line of fire," he chuckled, and Kathleen found herself warming to the pleasant sound.

"I generally choose an inanimate object as my target," she laughed. Her laughter was cut short by the sting of the disinfectant. She immediately leaned forward to try to get a better look at the injury to her foot. "It isn't very serious, is it?"

"No. It isn't as deep as it looks, but it's going to be sore to walk on. Did you actually believe you had a chance of catching that glass?" Jordan mocked gently, turning his head slightly toward her.

The hostility between them vanished. The well-formed mouth was inches away from her own. Kathleen was suddenly aware of how dangerously close it was, and her heart began drumming against her ribs at the darkening glow in his eyes. The force of his male attraction reached out to hold her captive.

As if he just realized that he had shed the chilling animosity, Jordan donned the cold mask of aloofness again. Quickly he smoothed the adhesive part of the bandage over her foot and straightened to his feet, severing that moment of bantering friendliness.

"From now on, I suggest that you wear your shoes," he said curtly.

He couldn't have made the dismissal any plainer if he had ordered her out of the room. Gingerly, Kathleen put her weight on her foot, favoring it slightly as she hobbled from his bedroom.

The shooting pain from her wound mingled with the pangs from his withdrawal. They were back to that uneasy truce. The brief, glimpse she had had of what it could be like between them made her dislike the state of cold war all the more.

At lunch on Saturday, Jordan announced that he wouldn't be home that evening. He was dining out, therefore Kathleen and the girls could plan the evening meal accordingly.

"Let's have pizza," Marsha suggested immediately.

"If you want," Kathleen agreed, smiling. She knew pizza would be the main course every night if Marsha had her way!

"Who are you going out with, dad?" Annette asked, pushing the cold cracked crab around on her plate with a fork.

"Kay Peters," he replied.

At the mention of the woman's name, Annette made a face of dislike as she glanced at Marsha. Kathleen saw it, but if Jordan noticed it he made no comment. And the subject was dropped.

That afternoon Jordan took the girls to the beach. Kathleen didn't go. Her cut was healing nicely and she didn't want to risk having infection set in. Instead she stayed at home and did the few pieces of ironing from the wash.

Barry called, asking if he could come out to see her that evening. Kathleen had put him off so many times that it was difficult to refuse him again. Besides, Jordan would be out for the evening. Since he had returned, she had been reluctant to have Barry come out, although she hadn't delved into the reason why she felt that way, even though Jordan had given his permission to have visitors.

So she told Barry to come around eight o'clock. Jordan would be gone by then. She also warned him that they wouldn't be able to go anywhere because of the girls. But he said he was content just to see her, and accepted the invitation.

Somehow Kathleen never got around to mentioning to Jordan that Barry was coming out. First of all the girls claimed most of her attention with their elaborate plans for pizza supreme. Then Jordan was in his room, showering and changing into evening clothes.

Before she knew it, he was gone and she hadn't told him. She tried to reconcile her guilty conscience with the fact that he had already given permission once and that she didn't need to obtain it again.

Barry arrived promptly at eight. The girls were openly curious about him, plaguing him with questions until Kathleen began to feel sorry for him and came to his rescue.

"Annette, why don't you and Marsha fix some popcorn and cold drinks for the four of us?" Kathleen suggested.

"Let's all go and fix it," Annette countered.

Kathleen slid a sideways glance at Barry, who smiled wryly and said, "Why not?"

With Annette organizing the project, they all trooped out to the kitchen. She had Marsha getting the popper out of the cupboard and adding the oil and popcorn. Barry was delegated to fill the glasses with ice cubes from the freezer while Kathleen made the tea and Annette melted the butter to pour over the popcorn.

When the last kernel had popped and the salt and butter had been sprinkled over the top, they all sat around the breakfast table in the kitchen, munching from individual bowls. The homey atmosphere put Barry at his ease.

"I haven't done this in years," he smiled at Kathleen. "Certainly not since I left home."

"It's fun, isn't it?" Annette chimed in. "Dad loves to fix popcorn, especially in the winter when it's cold and dreary outside, and we have a fire roaring in the fireplace. Then we'll sit around in the evening fixing popcorn or roasting marshmallows."

In one sense, it was difficult for Kathleen to visualize her somewhat sardonic employer in that light, but she had only to remember the glimpse she had had the other day and to picture his affectionate manner toward the girls to realize there was another side than the harsh one she usually saw.

"He's always doing things like that with us when he's at home," Marsha inserted.

"It sounds as if you have a close relationship with your father," Barry commented, and Kathleen knew the trace of envy in his tone was the result of his less than close relationship with his father. Barry had always felt he had been a disappointment to his parents.

"We do," Marsha assured him. "He used to say we were the Three Musketeers."

Kathleen wiped her buttery fingers on a paper napkin, suddenly curious what the girls thought of Jordan going out without them. "Does it bother you when he goes out for an evening?"

There was a quick, measuring flash of Annette's astute gray eyes. "You mean with some woman? No, it doesn't bother us. After all, he is a man," she declared in worldly tones. It was a point Kathleen would not dispute. "Actually, he dates quite frequently, although this is the first time he's gone out since you came to live with us, Kathleen."

"Have you girls ever met any of the women your father dates?" Barry asked the question that was uppermost in Kathleen's mind, although she was reluctant to voice it.

"Oh, yes," Annette nodded. "We go along sometimes when Father takes some woman to the beach or sailing."

"It must be nice for you girls to be included," Barry commented.

"It's awful," came the mumbled response from Marsha, who was staring grimly at her popcorn. "They always pat us on the head and tell us what pretty girls we are and what a wonderful father we have. They're all phoneys."

The vehement statement surprised Kathleen. She had never expected that type of jealous reaction from the two girls. They had always seemed so unselfish in their demands on their father.

"Actually," Annette explained with agreement, "Father's taste in women is abominable. Of course I've tried to explain to Marsha that he doesn't date them for companionship, but she's a little too young to understand, if you know what I mean."

She darted a knowing look at Kathleen, who found herself uncomfortably imagining Jordan making love to some Nordic blonde. Barry's hand was covering his mouth to hide a smile.

"Actually, I think the real reason he goes out with that type of woman is because he doesn't want to get married again," Annette continued, absently stirring the popcorn in the bowl with her fingers. "He's told us that he doesn't want to be tied down again and that we're all the permanent women he needs in his life. He doesn't seem to realize that in a few years we'll be grown up and he'll be all alone. We think he should get married again—not to anyone he's seeing now, heaven forbid!" She shuddered eloquently. "It would be nice if he married someone like you, Kathleen." At Kathleen's start of embarrassed surprise, Annette added, "She would have to be closer to his own age, of course."

61

"Yes, of course," Kathleen agreed somewhat self-consciously. The last thing she wanted to do was point out that twelve years was not exactly a gigantic gap between her and Jordan. Fourteen years separated her own parents.

Her position in the household was tenuous enough as it was. She didn't need the added burden of the girls thrusting her upon Jordan as their candidate for a perfect stepmother.

"I have a great idea!" Annette exclaimed, and Kathleen's heart stopped beating for a full second. "Let's all watch the late movie together." It started beating again, her pulse racing with relief. "It's supposed to be a really good horror film. It isn't a week night. We can stay up to watch it, can't we, Kathleen?"

"I don't see why not," Kathleen smiled.

"Come on, Marsha, let's clean up this mess." Annette was already scrambling from the table, taking the emptied tea glasses with her while Marsha stacked the bowls.

Later, as they were all making their way back to the living room, Barry murmured to Kathleen, "They're a precocious pair."

"Yes, and they're a lot of fun, too." Although sometimes, she thought silently, Annette's adultlike perception was unnerving.

"Don't turn out all the lights," Marsha protested as Annette switched on the television in the living room, then walked around turning off all the lights.

"It's better if the room is dark," Annette stated. "It sets the atmosphere for the movie."

"But it's scary when it's dark." Marsha curled into a ball in an overstuffed armchair, a circular green pillow clutched in her hands.

"I like being scared," Annette declared airily, taking a pillow from the couch and lying down on the floor in front of the television. "Besides, it's only a movie, and Kathleen and Barry are going to watch it with you."

As Kathleen sat on the couch beside Barry, she noted again the dissimilarity between the two girls, Annette the adventurous and Marsha the meek. Yet, despite their differences, they were remarkably close.

The movie was one of the better horror films, highlighted by stunning special effects. As the suspense and terror began building to the climactic conclusion, Barry bent his head toward Kathleen, his arm resting companionably around her shoulder.

"Take a look at Marsha," he whispered next to her ear. Kathleen's glance saw that Marsha had her face buried in the pillow, unable to watch what was happening. The background music of the film was rising to its crescendo. "She stayed awake all this time and now she's going to miss seeing the end!"

The overhead light was suddenly switched on, flooding the room with light. Marsha screamed and Annette sat up. Kathleen moved guiltily away from Barry's encircling arm even before she saw the tall, dark-haired man in the dining-room archway.

Gray eyes as cold and stormy as the Atlantic in winter were focused on her. She felt her cheeks pale under their piercing censure. Her mouth became parched.

"Dad!" Annette exclaimed with a sigh. "You shouldn't startle us like that. You just about scared Marsha to death."

"Shouldn't you girls be in bed? It's nearly one o'clock." His gaze flicked coldly and pointedly to Barry. There was nothing subtle in the silent message that it was time he left.

"Kathleen said we could stay up and watch the late movie," Annette explained, plumping her pillow and resuming her former position on the floor in front of the television. "It's nearly over."

Kathleen darted a hesitant, sideways glance at Barry. The arm that had been around her shoulders was now self-consciously at his side. She knew Barry had formed the impression that Jordan Long would be considerably older and less virilely handsome than the man glaring coldly at him now.

"I'm glad you're home, dad," Marsha murmured, letting the protective pillow fall to her lap.

"The End" flashed across the television screen and long strides carried Jordan to the set. "It's over now." He snapped off the set. "You girls get to bed."

"Oh, dad!" Annette grumbled, and rose to her feet.

Barry ran his fingers through the side of his hair. "It's late. I'd better be going, too."

"I'll walk you to the door," Kathleen murmured nervously, joining him as he straightened from the couch.

Jordan remained in the living room while the four of them entered the hall, the girls branching off toward the closed staircase and Kathleen and Barry moving toward the front door. Barry had seen the forbidding set of Jordan's jaw and accepted her rather hurried good night.

"I'll call you next week," he promised, and kissed her lightly on the cheek, then left.

Taking a deep breath, Kathleen closed and locked the front door, then turned around. Jordan was standing in the hall, darkly handsome in his evening suit.

"I take it that was your boyfriend." There was a faintly contemptuous ring to his voice.

"Yes, that was Barry." Kathleen tried to reply evenly. "Obviously he came to see me." Her response bordered on defiance, a defensive reaction to his intimidating manner.

"You knew he was coming?" It was really more of a condemning statement than a question.

"Yes," she admitted, lifting her chin a fraction of an inch.

"But you didn't mention it to me?"

"I didn't see the point." Kathleen shrugged self-consciously. "You'd already told me I could have visitors. I didn't think it was necessary to obtain your permission again, or to let you know in advance when they were calling."

His mouth tightened to a thin line. "At the time I gave you permission it didn't occur to me that your visitor would be male, or that you would be sitting with him on the couch necking in front of my daughters."

Kathleen breathed in sharply. "We were not necking!"

A black eyebrow arched arrogantly over the storm-cloud gray of his eyes. "You weren't?" he jeered. "I saw the way you were practically sitting on top of him when I walked in."

"I was not!" Her temper was fast reaching its boiling point. Muttering aloud, she started to walk past him, hoping to end the conversation before she lost control of her anger. "Of all the—"

His fingers dug into the soft flesh of her forearm. "Do you deny that he was nuzzling your neck?"

"I do!" she flashed. "Believe it or not, he was merely whispering something to me!"

"Really? What?" Jordan mocked. "Was he wanting you to hurry the girls off to bed so he could make love to you?"

Her free arm swung in a lightning arc toward his face, her open palm striking his cheek with a resounding slap. "You have a disgustingly vulgar mind!" she spat.

A savage anger glittered in his eyes, Kathleen had a moment to doubt the wisdom of her attack before an iron hand closed over hers.

With her hands straining against the solid wall of his chest, she tried to push herself away, but his superior strength overpowered her efforts and crushed her against his length. The harsh imprint of his muscular body against the softer curves of Kathleen's weakened her resistance.

The involuntary surrender brought a sensual change to the bruising pressure of his mouth. Its firm yet persuasive touch started a wildfire that raged through her veins. The devouring flames made her pliant to his demands. Expertly Jordan parted her lips, and she shuddered with uncontrollable desire at his intimate exploration. The arousing caress of his hand over her back and hips arched her even closer to him, molding her flesh to his.

THE STAIRWELL DOOR in the entry hall was partially open. Like two little mice, Annette and Marsha sneaked down the stairs, slinking along the edge of the steps so the boards wouldn't creak and betray their presence.

Annette crouched on the lowest step, while Marsha leaned forward above her to peer through the crack between the door and its frame. They both spied the embracing couple at the same time. Marsha straightened away from the door in embarrassed surprise, while Annette watched for a second longer.

Quickly but silently, Annette straightened and motioned for her sister to go back upstairs. Not until they reached the top did she let the excitement burst from her.

"It's working!" Annette whispered gleefully. "I told you it would."

"But he was so angry when he came home." A puzzled frown creased Marsha's forehead as she tried to understand.

"It doesn't matter what he was like when he came home." Annette shook her head impatiently. "That was a kiss of passion if I ever saw one."

Marsha tilted her dark head. "Have you ever seen one?"

Conveniently Annette ignored the question, holding a finger to her lips. "Ssh, I thought I heard something," she whispered. "We'd better go to our rooms, just in case Kathleen is on her way up."

WHEN JORDAN LIFTED HIS HEAD, Kathleen remained motionless, her fingers desperately clutching the lapels of his jacket. Her eyes were closed, her lips moist and trembling from his kiss. Her senses were still reeling from the passionate assault that had shaken her nearly to the very core of her being.

"Now, Miss Darrow—" his sarcastic voice spilled over her like an icy bucket of water "—convince me that you wouldn't want a man to make love to you if you were alone with him."

For a frozen second, she could only blink at him in disbelief. Then the shame of how abandonedly she had responded to his embrace washed over her with sobering force. Wrenching free of his hold, she raced for the stairs, humiliated beyond words that she had let him see how susceptible she was to his advance. If his opinion of her had been low before, it was even lower now.

7

S unday was a difficult day. Although Jordan didn't make a single reference to the embarrassing episode the night before, it remained foremost in Kathleen's thoughts. She couldn't look at him without her gaze being drawn to his well-formed mouth and remembering the way it had demolished her inhibitions.

Later in the afternoon, Jordan had left to drive to the Greater Wilmington Airport. He was flying to Louisiana to straighten out some regulation problems on one of the offshore rigs. It was his last assignment before his vacation officially began.

Kathleen had volunteered to drive him to the airport, but he had declined her offer, preferring to leave his car at the airport so he would have transport when he returned. Since Kathleen had her Volkswagen, it was a practical arrangement.

The week dragged by very slowly. Her reaction to its slowness was ambivalent. On one hand, she dreaded the approaching weekend when Jordan would return, wanting to prolong the harmonious days with the girls.

On the other, she wanted to get the month's trial over, an agreement she wished now she hadn't made.

She had arranged with Mrs. Long to have Wednesday off. She had left the girls at their great-aunt's and had spent the better part of the day with Maggie, who had relayed all the latest gossip at the hospital to Kathleen.

There had been no phone calls from Jordan. When he had left, he had stated only that he would be home the following weekend, not naming a specific day.

On Sunday, Kathleen and the girls drove into town to go to church with Mrs. Long. Then Kathleen invited her to have Sunday dinner with them and spend the afternoon. She wondered if she wasn't subconsciously trying to insulate herself against Jordan's arrival. When the dinner dishes had been washed and put away, the girls had brought out their Monopoly board and set it up on the kitchen table. Kathleen hadn't been able to concentrate on the game as she constantly listened for the sound of Jordan's car pulling into the garage.

Within a half an hour, she was bankrupt and out of the game. She remained seated at the table for a time, but was too restless and on edge to sit idly and watch. She doubted that the three players even noticed when she left the table.

There was a half-formed decision to change out of her Sunday dress. It was one of the more feminine garments in her wardrobe, a light, summery material in an apricot color with an accordion-pleated skirt that curled slightly at the hem.

In the entry hall, Kathleen remembered that the bulb in the hanging lamp overhead had burnt out. She had intended to replace the light bulb this morning, since it provided the only light in the hall, but had forgotten to do it.

Before she could forget a second time and be forced to replace it in the dark, she retraced her steps to the kitchen. There was gleeful laughter from Marsha when Annette landed on her Park Place. Amidst the confusion, Kathleen took a new bulb from the cupboard and walked, back to the entry hall, pausing in the dining room to carry one of the chairs with her so she could reach the lamp.

Setting the bulb on a side table, she positioned the chair under the hanging lamp. Afraid that the heels of her shoes would catch in the needlepoint cushion of the chair, she slipped them off and climbed onto the chair seat.

Stretching on tiptoes, she could just reach the burnt out bulb.

As she started unscrewing the bulb, the front door opened, and her hazel eyes darted to Jordan in surprise. A few more turns and the bulb would be free. She didn't dare let go of it or it might crash to the floor, yet she couldn't tear her gaze from him or move from her position.

67

Dressed in a dark business suit and tie, he stepped into the hall, closing the front door behind him. His compelling features were etched with tiredness as he set his briefcase and luggage on the floor. Kathleen's heart was doing all sorts of crazy acrobatics at the way the gray eyes were mercilessly examining her from head to toe, dwelling for several seconds on the shapely length of her legs below the skirt of her dress.

His mouth quirked cynically. "I see you chose to ignore my advice."

"Advice?" Kathleen echoed blankly. There was a tremor in her voice at the disturbing gray light in his eyes.

"No shoes." His gaze flicked pointedly to her stockinged feet.

Another turn and the bulb was free. Auburn hair fell forward across her cheeks as she stepped down from the chair and walked to the side table for the new bulb.

"You'll have to blame my mother." She avoided looking at him as she removed the bulb from its protective cardboard container. "She taught me never to climb on furniture with shoes on." Trying to change the subject, she asked, "Why did you come in the front?"

"Because your car was blocking the garage door," he answered dryly.

She flushed guiltily. "I'm sorry."

"So you would rather risk cutting a foot than getting a little dirt on the chair," mocked Jordan, reverting to the original subject without acknowledging her apology.

Kathleen walked back to the chair, stepping onto the seat with a hand on the wooden back for balance. She was aware by the direction of his low voice that he had moved closer. When she raised her arm to insert the new bulb, he was in front of her.

His hands gripped the sides of her waist. Automatically, she lowered her arms to his shoulders for support. He lifted her from the chair to the floor, holding her there for an instant while Kathleen's senses quivered with his nearness.

A sardonic smile was carved into his compelling features. "Put your shoes on so there won't be a need for any more first aid," he ordered firmly. "I'll put the bulb in."

There was a weakness in her knees as she bent to retrieve her shoes. Aware of his power to disturb her physically, Kathleen moved well away from the chair. With a few expert turns, Jordan had the new light bulb in the socket and was stepping down from the chair.

"Where are the girls?" His hand brushed the ebony blackness of his hair to one side, a gesture that seemed to accentuate his tiredness.

"In the kitchen playing Monopoly with Helen," Kathleen answered, picking up the dining-room chair to return it.

"Helen?" Jordan frowned. "Do you mean my aunt?"

"Yes, we all went to church together, then I invited her out here for dinner with us," she explained, adding as an afterthought, "there's some cold roast left. Could I make you a sandwich?"

"Maybe later." He shrugged aside her offer and walked toward the kitchen.

Kathleen followed more slowly, taking her time in replacing the chair at the dining-room table. Finally she could delay no longer and entered the room where the excited girls were welcoming their father. The Monopoly game had been forgotten. She managed to stay pretty well in the background until Helen Long suggested it was time she went home.

"I'll take you," Kathleen volunteered.

Marsha was standing beside the kitchen chair where Jordan was sitting, her arm partially around his wide shoulders. He glanced up at her and smiled, a faintly weary movement.

"Why don't you two girls ride along with Kathleen?" he suggested. "That way I can shower and change without interruptions while you're gone."

Several minutes later, the four of them were all in Kathleen's small car. They stayed for only a few minutes at Helen's home to make sure everything was all right, then drove straight back. This time Kathleen parked her car well clear of the garage door.

It was just as close for them to use the front door as it was to walk to the kitchen entrance through the garage. Jordan's luggage was still sitting inside the door along with his briefcase. Kathleen sent Annette to the kitchen to clear away the Monopoly game and to start preparing a cold supper. She gave the briefcase to Marsha, assuming that Jordan would want it in his study.

The luggage she carried down the hall to the master bedroom. There was no sound of movement inside the room. She knocked once on the door and it swung open. Jordan was lying in the center of the bed, his suit jacket thrown carelessly to one side. He was asleep.

Quietly, Kathleen walked in and set his luggage on the floor at the foot of the bed. She hesitated, glancing at the sleeping figure. The only thing he had removed was his jacket. He still had on his shoes and his shirt was buttoned all the way, with the tie still knotted at his throat.

Taking care not to waken him, she untied his shoes and eased them off his feet. Loosening his tie was a more difficult task. He was sleeping in the center of the oversize bed, too far from the edge for Kathleen to lean over the bed and reach him.

Lowering her weight onto the bed, she carefully began loosening the knot of his tie. He stirred once, and she waited, holding her breath. When he lay quietly again, her fingers resumed their work on the knot.

"Were you planning on strangling me in my sleep?" Jordan murmured unexpectedly, his voice thick with exhaustion.

Her startled gaze flew to his face. Black lashes were partially raised, allowing a mere slit of an opening for his charcoal-gray eyes to see her. For an instant, Kathleen was shaken by his discovery of what she was doing, then a professional calm took over.

"I was trying to loosen your tie so you could sleep more comfortably," she explained evenly, and continued her task.

The lashes closed, accompanied by a suggestion of a tired sigh. His right hand moved up as if to join hers. Instead it began unbuttoning his shirt, starting with the middle buttons so as not to interfere with her effort to loosen his tie.

"I didn't make it to the shower," Jordan stated the obvious. "I never got past the bed."

With the tie free of its knot, Kathleen undid the top buttons. "You were tired," she said softly. A smile curved her mouth. She had never expected to see the formidable Jordan Long look so vulnerable.

His hand fell away and she unbuttoned the rest of the buttons. With practiced ease, she turned him on his side and slipped off half of his shirt and turned him on the other side to free it completely.

There was a whimsical curve to his mouth when he was lying once again on his back, his eyes still closed. "It's been a long time since a woman has undressed me," he murmured. "You're very expert at it."

"I'm a nurse, remember?" She stopped with the shirt. But she was well aware of the fact that she did not possess the necessary detachment where Jordan was concerned.

One bronzed shoulder moved against the mattress in a stretching motion. "I haven't slept in thirty-six hours and my muscles feel like high tension coils." A slit of gray focused on her again. "I don't suppose your training as a nurse included rub-downs?"

Kathleen could see the corded tautness and nodded. "I had a course in physiotherapy."

He rolled toward her onto his stomach, taking her statement as an agreement to massage his tense and aching muscles. The movement brought him closer to the edge of the bed, and Kathleen was able to stand on the floor while her hands kneaded his tautly muscled back.

After several minutes his respiration became slow and steady, and she guessed he had drifted back to sleep.

Under the administering massage, of her fingers, some of the tenseness had left, but not all. Annette appeared in the open doorway, and Kathleen held a finger to her lips to indicate silence. Annette nodded, smiling widely, and retreated to another part of the house.

When Jordan rolled away from her onto his back, Kathleen stopped, but he seemed about to waken, so she put a knee on the bed and began slowly rubbing his upper arms and shoulders. The position was awkward, and she began to tire.

As if he felt her firm touch faltering, Jordan reached up to lightly clasp her left hand in his right, sooty lashes lifting to gaze at her. Her leaning position had her balanced precariously above him.

"That's enough." The smoky light in his eyes thanked her. "Did anyone ever tell you that you have magic fingers?"

Her auburn hair had been tucked behind her ears. One side slid free, falling across her cheek and shimmering with a dark fire. For an instant she wanted to ignore his statement that she had done enough and let her hands continue their unrestricted exploration of his hard chest and arms. But it was simply too dangerous.

"No, I haven't been told that before." She shook her head and would have straightened.

His right hand reached up and smoothed the hair behind her ear. The unexpected caress checked her movement away from him. His fingers remained along the side of her neck. The darkening light in his eyes made her heart leap suddenly.

Exerting the slightest pressure, Jordan pulled her head toward him. Caught in the magnetic pull of his animal attraction, it didn't even occur to Kathleen to resist.

Warm and languid, his mouth closed over hers, kindling a slow-burning flame in her midsection that grew steadily hotter.

Her fingers spread themselves over the granite strength of his chest, encountering the curling dark hairs that tickled her palms. His hand slid between her shoulder blades, drawing her down to the nakedness of his torso. An avalanche of churning desires coursed through her, stimulated by the seductive mastery of his hard male lips.

There was no urgency to his caress. It was languorous and slow, as if they had all the time in the world. His left hand moved sensuously down her waist to the curve of her hip and along her thigh, entangling itself in the soft folds of her skirt. The erotic male scent of him filled her senses. Primitive yearnings surfaced with a rush.

Her skirt was pushed carelessly out of the way by his hand as it explored her silken-clad thigh. The arousing touch succeeded in awakening her to the danger of her actions. She turned her head away from the drugging ecstasy of his mouth, quivering with the fullness of her response.

"Please." But he focused his attention on the throbbing vein in her neck. "Don't!" She tried to push herself away. With a slight twist of pressure, Jordan forced her onto the bed beside him, her head resting on his shoulder.

"Stay with me." The order was issued in a low voice husky with passion.

"No." It was a protest against how very much she wanted to stay, against how very successfully he made her want to stay. She tried to recapture her sanity. "Jordan, don't do this."

Deliberately he tantalized her mouth, letting his lips play near one corner of it. "Say my name again."

"Jordan," Kathleen moaned softly, almost sinking again under his spell. Then his hand moved to rest lightly on the curve of her breast. With the last of her willpower, she slid free of his arms to the edge of the bed. On shaking legs, she took a step away. "Mr. Long—" her voice trembled traitorously "—you're tired and need sleep."

The smoldering light in his eyes studied her, a suggestion of labored breathing in the rise and fall of his tanned chest. Then he seemed to relax against the covers.

"Yes," he agreed simply.

Pivoting, Kathleen hurried through the doorway into the hall. There was no sensation of relief, only a lingering taste of bitter disappointment, which did nothing to bolster her serf-respect.

No man's touch had ever turned her bones to jelly before. The possibility that it might be more than physical attraction, that she might be falling in love with Jordan, did not fill her with gladness. How could it when he had done nothing but insult and accuse her of all sorts of trickery since they had first met?

A glimpse of her reflection in a hall mirror told her that she didn't dare rejoin the girls in her present state. Her auburn hair was rumpled and disheveled. There was a flush to her cheeks, and her lips were slightly swollen from Jordan's seductive kisses. Her appearance was a definite betrayal of her passionate romp on the bed only moments before.

Altering her direction, she walked toward the stairwell door. A quick wash and change of clothes was needed. Her hand closed over the doorknob and started to turn it.

"Kathleen?"

She nearly jumped out of her shoes at the sound of Annette's voice. A deeper scarlet stain spread over her face and neck as she turned in answer.

"Yes?" Her voice was brittle. The professional poise she usually could summon had deserted her.

The young girl's sweeping study of her was unnerving. "I have a cold supper all set out."

"Good." Kathleen couldn't even force a smile. "Why don't you girls go ahead and fix a sandwich? Your father is sleeping." A nervous hand ran lightly over the front of her skirt. "I was going upstairs to change. I...I'll be right down."

"Okay." Innocent gray eyes blinked an agreement before Annette turned to reenter the living room.

ANNETTE WAS SPRAWLED crosswise over an armchair, watching a Disney wildlife documentary on television with interest. Marsha sat crosslegged on the floor in front of the television, equally engrossed in the program.

The sound of firm strides shifted Annette's attention to the hall, without changing her position. She smiled somewhat absently when her father appeared. "Hi, dad," she greeted him. "We were beginning to think you'd sleep until morning."

The lines of tiredness had left his strong features. His ebony hair gleamed wetly, a sure indication, along with his fresh appearance, that he had just showered. A pair of blue knit slacks hugged his muscular thighs and slim hips, complemented by a patterned silk shirt that molded the breadth of his chest.

An absent frown of disapproval drew his dark brows together as he glanced at his older daughter. "Chairs are for sitting, Annette, not lying." Grimacing, she swung her legs off the chair arm and sat up. His charcoal gaze swept the living room. "Where's Kathleen?"

A knowing sparkle entered Annette's lighter gray eyes, but it was Marsha who answered. "She's in the kitchen washing up the supper dishes."

A dark brow shot up. "Shouldn't you be helping?"

"Not on Sunday," Marsha explained, her attention not diverted from the television. "It's our day off. Kathleen says we're entitled to one, too."

"There's plenty of food left if you're hungry," Annette suggested. "We didn't know how long you'd sleep, so we put it all away, but Kathleen will fix you something if you ask her."

Jordan didn't reply to that, but walked through the living room to the dining room. His destination was obviously the kitchen. Annette watched him from her chair, waiting until she heard the swinging of the door into the kitchen before she moved to follow. Marsha glanced at her curiously.

"You wait here." Annette waved a detaining hand at her. "I'm just going to see what's happening."

Marsha shrugged and looked back at the television while Annette stole silently into the dining room, pausing beside the door to the kitchen and cocking her head in a listening manner.

KATHLEEN RINSED A PLATE under the tap and set it on the draining-board. At the opening of the door, she glanced absently over her shoulder, expecting to see one of the girls. For a startled instant, her hazel eyes met the piercing steel gray of Jordan's.

Her pulse rocketed, but luckily she had had time to rebuild her shattered composure and was able to look away with commendable blandness. The dishcloth wiped another plate in the sudsy water.

"There's cold meat and salad in the refrigerator if you're hungry," she offered.

Jordan's gaze bored holes in her back for several seconds. "That isn't why I'm here," he stated cryptically.

He walked to the counter beside the sink where Kathleen was washing dishes. Although he was within her line of vision, she didn't glance at him, but her senses were raised to a fever pitch of awareness. Soap and after-shave lotion mingling with the musky scent of his maleness made an intoxicating combination. Her nerve ends vibrated at his nearness.

"What was it you wanted?" Did that cool and calm voice belong to her? Kathleen marveled silently.

"I owe you an apology." His gaze compelled her to look at him. She did so, reluctantly. His aloof regard was almost freezing. "The only excuse I have for my behavior earlier this evening is that I was excessively tired."

"I understand."

Bitterness again welled in her throat. She understood very well. He probably would have asked any woman to stay. Kathleen just happened to be the one who was there.

Jordan seemed to find her acknowledgment of his apology less than acceptable and his expression hardened. "I am not in the habit of making amorous advances to female employees, Kathleen," he scowled.

It would have been much easier to maintain his piercing gaze if he had addressed her more formally. As it was, Kathleen had to look away. The sight of his mouth forming her name was disturbing.

"I never supposed you did, Mr. Long," she replied.

A muscle twitched along his jawline at her formal reference to him. Her hands were remarkably steady as she continued washing the dishes and rinsing them under the tap.

"I also wanted to assure you that there wouldn't be a repetition of that regrettable incident," Jordan said tersely.

Kathleen paused, indignation rising within her. He didn't have to make it quite so plain that he wasn't interested in her. She had not misinterpreted his actions.

"I'm an adult and a nurse." She spoke slowly and concisely, anger trembling on the edge of her voice. "I'm aware that physical urges don't necessarily reflect personal likes or dislikes. As far as I'm concerned the human lapse, on both our parts, has been forgotten." It was a blatant lie, but there was little else she could say if she wanted to save her pride.

74

His gaze narrowed on her profile, measuring the amount of truth in her words. Kathleen tossed her head back, dark red fire gleaming from the silken curls of her hair, as she met his hard gaze without flinching.

"I'm glad we understand one another," he said finally. "There's something else I wanted to discuss with you."

She turned back to the sink full of sudsy water, unconsciously squaring her shoulders. What was left to talk about, she asked herself?

Aloud, she merely said, "Yes?"

"Under the circumstances, I believe it's pointless to carry out this month's trial," Jordan declared.

Her heart sank to her toes. "I couldn't agree with you more," she replied bravely. "If you like, I'll pack and leave in the morning."

"I didn't mean to end it that abruptly." There was a humorless twist to his mouth. "What I had planned to suggest was that I begin interviewing a replacement, if that meets with your approval. You may stay on until I find one or you may leave. The girls and I can make do."

Kathleen moistened, her lips, wishing her heart hadn't leaped so wildly at the brief reprieve. "I was under the impression that you would prefer I left immediately," she defended her previous comment.

"Not necessarily," he qualified. "Since we're both aware of the complications that could arise from living together in such close and intimate proximity, I believe we both can avoid any further uncomfortable situations in the next few days."

"Of course." There was a tight lump in her throat. "In that case, I'll stay."

She stared down at her hands and the dishcloth that she was clutching in her fingers. "Will you tell the girls immediately?"

There was a second's hesitation, and she darted a quick glance at the grim hard line of his mouth.

They were both aware of the way the two girls felt toward her. His decision would certainly not be popular.

"Not immediately." There was a snap of impatience in his voice. "Not until I've decided on a replacement. There isn't any need for them to get upset in advance. I'll contact the employment agency tomorrow and arrange for the interviews to be held in their offices."

"That would be best, I suppose," Kathleen agreed. A fleetingly poignant smile touched her mouth. Whoever her replacement turned out to be, she would never experience the wonder of being interviewed by two adolescents.

"What's the matter?" Jordan questioned her brief smile.

"I was just remembering the first time I met Annette and Marsha."

75

She shrugged, and earnestly began washing the rest of the dishes.
He studied her silently, then walked to the refrigerator.

ANNETTE STRAIGHTENED away from the door. "Good grief" she muttered as she
stalked back toward the living room. Draping herself over the armchair, she
began thoughtfully nibbling at her lower lip. Somehow she had to think of a
way to stop her father.

8

The two girls were huddled together outside the study door, a blond head bent confidently toward the shorter dark-haired girl.

"Now, remember," Annette whispered, "don't let anyone pick up the telephone extension in the living room. And if it looks as if dad is heading for the study, you'll have to sidetrack him somehow."

"How?"

"I don't know how," Annette sighed impatiently. "Take him outside to see what's wrong with your bike."

"But there isn't anything wrong with my bike."

"Don't be so obtuse! *Pretend* there's something wrong with your bike!" Her hands waved the air at the sheer hopelessness of her sister.

"Okay," Marsha grumbled.

With a surreptitious glance to be sure no one was watching, Annette slipped into the study, quietly closing the door behind her. She walked hurriedly to the desk, looked up a telephone number in the directory and dialed. Her fingers drummed the desktop as she waited for an answer.

"The business office, please," she requested in her oldest voice. There was another pause. "Yes, this is Mrs. Long. I would like to request that this number be temporarily disconnected for a month while we are on vacation...That's correct. I would like it done immediately—today—this morning...I realize it's very short notice, but surely you can arrange it...You can? By ten o'clock. Thank you very much."

A gleam of satisfaction was in her gray eyes as she replaced the telephone receiver. She sighed, then smiled widely, rising from the desk chair.

"Well, we've postponed that for a couple of days anyway," Annette murmured to herself. "Now for plan B."

At the door to the hall, she could hear voices. One of them was Marsha's. Crossing her fingers, she waited silently beside the door. Then there was the sound of the front door opening and closing, and Annette exhaled the breath she had been holding with relief. She slipped quickly back into the hall and out the front door.

"There you are!" she called out, as if in surprise, when she saw her father wheeling Marsha's bike out of the garage. "What are you doing?"

"Marsha said there was something wrong with her bike," Jordan replied.

"Her chain was slipping the other day," Annette said, backing up her sister's fib.

He studied the chain for a few minutes, testing it out. "It seems to be all right now."

"I did try to tighten it—" Annette spoke up again as Marsha shifted uncomfortably beside her father "—but I wasn't sure if I'd fixed it."

"It looks as if you did." He straightened. "You can put it back in the garage, Marsha."

"Kathleen should have breakfast ready. I heard her out in the kitchen." Annette started walking toward the garage and the side entrance.

"I'll be joining you shortly," said Jordan. "There's a phone call I want to make first."

"It can wait until after breakfast," Annette argued, holding her breath. "You know how much you dislike cold eggs, dad. Besides, you're on vacation, remember? So your phone call can't be that important."

He hesitated, then smiled rather tightly. "No, I suppose it can wait for another hour."

Annette glanced at Marsha, the flicker of her lashes indicating her relief.

JORDAN WALKED OUT OF THE STUDY into the living room and picked up the telephone extension there. He replaced the receiver after a minute and frowned.

"What's the matter, dad?" Annette looked at him blankly.

"The telephone is dead." He glanced at Kathleen. "I don't understand. Have there been any electrical shortages or storms?"

"No. It was working yesterday morning when I called Helen," she answered.

78

"It's out of order now," Jordan stated, moving to the side door into the garage. "I'll have to drive to the service station on the highway and use their phone to report it."

"We'll ride along with you to keep you company, dad," Annette said, following him and pushing Marsha in front of her.

He hesitated at the door. "There's no need for you girls to come along."

The blond cap of hair was tipped to the side as Annette replied, "But we want to."

Jordan's gaze sought Kathleen's over the top of the girl's heads. She knew the cause of his indecision. After reporting the trouble with their telephone, he had intended to call the employment agency, and with the girls along, there was a chance they would overhear. Yet it would be churlish for him to refuse to let them accompany him.

She tried to come to his rescue. "I thought you girls were going to bake cookies this morning."

"We can do that when we get back," Annette shrugged offhandedly. "We aren't going to be gone that long." She turned back to her father, a frown creasing her forehead. "What's the matter? Don't you want us, daddy?"

There was a brief tightening of his mouth before he smiled. "Of course I do. Come on."

Twenty minutes later they were back with the information that the telephone repair man would be out late that afternoon or Tuesday morning. He didn't show up at either time, so on Tuesday afternoon Jordan drove back to report the delay and find out why. The girls went with him.

They were considerably longer coming back, and one look at the forbidding set of Jordan's expression when he walked through the door told Kathleen that someone at the telephone company had received the sharp edge of his tongue.

"Are they sending a repair man out?" she asked.

"They don't need to," he answered cryptically.

"You'll never believe what happened!" Annette exclaimed.

"What?" Kathleen glanced curiously at Jordan, who had walked to the counter to pour himself a cup of coffee.

"The telephone company received a request to temporarily disconnect the service while we were on vacation," he explained tersely.

"Can you believe that?" Annette shook her head and walked to the cookie jar.

"A request? From whom?" Kathleen frowned.

His dark gray eyes slid briefly to her, faintly measuring and guarded. "From some woman claiming to be Mrs. Long," he answered.

Jordan didn't actually think she had done it, did he? What reason did she have? Kathleen protested silently. Surely he didn't believe she had done it to prevent him from contacting the employment agency? She had volunteered to leave immediately without waiting for him to hire a replacement.

"There must have been some mix-up," she said aloud. "The request could have been meant for some other family in the area named Long."

"Possibly," he agreed.

"Or else it was some weirdo's idea of a practical joke," Annette suggested, biting into a sugar cookie.

"Either way, the service will be restored this morning," Jordan announced.

Annette walked over to lean against the counter beside Marsha.

"What are we going to do today, dad?"

"Nothing, until I make certain the phone is working again."

Out of the corner of her eye, Kathleen saw the sharp nudge Annette gave Marsha with her elbow. For a moment, Marsha looked at her sister blankly, then turned to her father.

"If we can't go anywhere today, then tomorrow can we go to Rehoboth Beach?" Marsha inquired hesitantly.

He seemed to consider the suggestion for a moment, then nodded. "I don't see why not," he agreed. "We can make a day of it and let Kathleen have tomorrow as her free time this week."

"Oh, no!" Annette's protest was immediate. "I meant for all four of us to go together," forgetting that it was Marsha who had made the initial suggestion at the prompting of Annette's elbow.

Jordan flashed another look at Kathleen. "I think not."

"But, dad—" Annette wasn't giving up "—you know how you hate wandering through the shops along the boardwalk. It would be so much more fun for Marsha and me if Kathleen went along. Besides, she hasn't had her weekend off yet this month, so really her free time this week should be Saturday and Sunday. That was the agreement when she came to work here."

"Very well." The darkening gray eyes made no attempt to disguise his displeasure even as he consented to make the outing a foursome.

While she disliked the idea of being the unwanted fourth as far as Jordan was concerned, Kathleen knew she needed the weekend to begin making arrangements for the day when she would no longer be working there. She had sublet her apartment and now was faced with the unwelcome task of finding another, as well as a new job.

Shortly after midmorning the next day, they arrived at the resort town on the Atlantic coast of Delaware. The day was warm, the sky an opaque blue. The car was parked in a lot near the beach, a picnic hamper in the back.

The girls decreed that the first order of the day was a stroll along the beach's boardwalk to investigate the shops. True to Annette's comment,

Jordan waited for them outside the various shop doors while Kathleen and the girls perused the wares to their hearts' content.

Before long, Kathleen's vague apprehensions about the outing had fled. The lighthearted spirit of the two girls was contagious. Soon even Jordan's aloofness was fading under the charm of their enthusiasm. With it, Kathleen's wariness whenever he was with them began to disappear, too. As if for the girls' benefit, they established a friendly rapport.

They had just stepped out of a shop and rejoined Jordan when Annette breathed in deeply. "What is that? It smells delicious," she declared.

Kathleen sniffed the aromatic scent and sighed in instant recognition. "Hot pretzels," she identified it, immediately seeking the location of the vendor. "There it is."

"Let's buy some," Annette suggested.

"Later," said Jordan. "You'll spoil your appetite for the picnic lunch Kathleen's brought."

"Not if we just have one apiece," Kathleen protested, lifting her head to look at him.

As he gazed down at her upturned face, low laughter broke from his throat. "I believe you want one more than the girls!"

A dimpling smile curved her mouth, vivid flecks of green in her hazel eyes. "I do," she admitted with rueful amusement. "I have a weakness for those fat pretzels still warm from the oven."

"Come on, dad," Annette coaxed. "We'll work up our appetite again just walking back to the car."

"How about you, Marsha? Do you want one, too?" Jordan smiled at his youngest daughter.

"Yes," she nodded with shy eagerness.

"I'm outnumbered, then." He acquiesced with mock resignation.

They joined the line at the vendor's window, waiting their turn as they inhaled the mouthwatering aroma emanating from the stand. Minutes later they were strolling down the boardwalk, each holding a warm, oversized pretzel, the brown crust frosted with yellow mustard.

Annette glanced over her shoulder, her gaze encompassing both Jordan and Kathleen walking behind her.

"Mmm, they're delicious," she declared appreciatively between mouthfuls.

"I could eat a dozen," Marsha agreed.

"Then you definitely wouldn't have any room for lunch." Jordan chuckled. "Considering the time Kathleen spent fixing it, she might not like it if we didn't eat." He slid Kathleen an amused sideways glance. The smile on his mouth deepened with disturbing force as he clicked his tongue at her in mock reproof. "You're as bad as the girls," he accused.

"Why?" Kathleen blinked, her tongue darting out to lick the mustard from her lips.

"You have mustard smeared from ear to ear." Silvery bright eyes crinkled at the corners when Kathleen stopped and quickly began wiping the edges of her mouth with a paper napkin. "Let me do it," Jordan insisted with an underlying tone of amused indulgence.

He took the napkin from her hand. Her mouth opened to protest, but he was already rubbing the paper with rough gentleness over her cheek. A self-conscious pink glow tinted her skin at the faint intimacy of his action. Yet Jordan seemed unconcerned. Kathleen hardly dared breathe in case she inadvertently let him see that even this casual gesture set off minor shock waves of awareness.

But her tenseness must have been transmitted to him. The paper against her cheek suddenly stopped its wiping motion. Unwillingly, she peered upward through her lashes, focusing on the cleft in his strong chin, then the immobile line of his mouth, upwards past his straight nose to the eagle sharpness of his eyes. They smoldered over her for an intoxicating instant before they turned a bleak, stormy gray.

Simultaneously his hand left her cheek, and he turned away. "That should do it," was his gruffly issued comment.

Her stomach was twisted in knots. How foolish she had been to believe even for a minute that she might spend a day in his company without being aware of him in a physical way. The attraction he held for her was too strong.

Miserably Kathleen felt little consolation in knowing she affected him in the same way, since he so plainly regretted it. The pretzel had lost its flavor, and it was only with a great deal of determination that she was able to finish the rest of it.

The curio shops, the clothing stores, with their window displays of beach wear, and the restaurants lining one side of the boardwalk all melted into a sameness in Kathleen's vision. The opposite view of ocean waves rolling onto the golden sand beach didn't seem any different. She kept walking along the planked boards, but without the inner gladness she had known a few minutes ago. Jordan was again withdrawn and reserved.

When they reached the car, Annette suggested they get the hamper and choose the place on the beach where they would have their picnic. As Jordan took the picnic hamper from the rear seat of the car the owners of the car parked next to them returned. The woman paused beside him, glancing warmly at the two girls and Kathleen waiting in front of the car.

"You have a lovely family," she commented with a beaming smile. "Your two daughters will be as beautiful as your wife when they grow up."

Jordan stiffened, then nodded with a trace of curtness. "Thank you."

Kathleen turned toward the ocean as he approached, a crimson stain dotting her cheeks. It would have been pointless for him to take the time to deny that she was his wife. The woman had been a total stranger who had been merely complimenting him on his daughters. Still, Kathleen wished that Jordan had told the woman the truth.

"Fancy that," Annette murmured. "That woman thought Kathleen was our mother, didn't she, dad?"

"Yes," he said tersely, and Kathleen cringed inwardly at his harsh tone.

"I wish she was," Marsha added quietly.

Kathleen wished she was an ostrich and could bury her head in the sand. There was too much twisting pain inside for her to see any humor in the situation. Marsha's comment hovered in the air, pressing heavily over the ensuing silence.

"Actually," Annette began thoughtfully, "I think we get most of our looks from you, dad." Her clear gray eyes shifted to Kathleen, who was walking beside her on the sand. "He is very handsome, don't you think?"

Swallowing the tight lump in her throat, Kathleen smiled nervously. "Yes, he is."

"Of course you're very pretty, too," Annette added quickly, as if she was afraid that she might have offended her. Just as quickly she changed the subject. "This looks like a good place for our picnic. Let's have it here."

Jordan obligingly set the hamper on the sand, while Annette and Marsha began spreading out the blanket. Kathleen made a pretense of checking the contents of the hamper to avoid looking at Jordan. With the blanket in place, Annette sat crosslegged on one corner.

Again her thoughtful gaze rested on Kathleen. "It would be nice if you were our stepmother." Then she sighed. "It's a pity that dad is so much older, otherwise the two of you could get married."

"There isn't that much difference in our ages," Jordan snapped.

Annette tipped her head back to gaze up at him. "You don't think so?" she inquired innocently.

"No, I don't," he retorted, a little less abruptly than before. "But it doesn't alter the fact that I'm not going to get married just to provide you girls with a stepmother."

"That would be silly!" Annette declared with an exasperated glance at her father. "People get married because they're in love, and you're not in love with Kathleen."

"Annette, please," Kathleen inserted with a brittle laugh, "this kind of talk is embarrassing to your father and me."

"Is it?" She looked startled. "Gosh, I'm sorry. Actually I was just trying to make conversation."

"I suggest you choose another topic," Jordan snapped. He flashed a piercing gray look at Kathleen that was onimously harsh and forbidding. Briskly it slashed to the silent Marsha. "Let's walk down by the water, Marsha," he ordered. "Kathleen and Annette can call us when the lunch is ready."

It was a long, uncomfortable afternoon. By the time they returned to the house, Kathleen's nerves were so raw from the strain that she wanted to collapse. Of course, she couldn't, not until the picnic things were washed and put away, a light supper had been served and the dishes done. Only then could she retreat to the security of her room, letting Jordan have the responsibility of the girls for the rest of the evening.

"I WISH I COULD UNDERSTAND what's going on in dad's mind," Annette grumbled as she changed into her scarlet swimsuit.

"What do you mean?" Marsha sat on the bed, already dressed in her blue swimsuit and twirling her bathing cap by its strap.

"He's hardly been civil to Kathleen since we went to Rehoboth Beach. And you know the way he practically bit our heads off if we even mentioned her name over the weekend," Annette sighed.

"I think he hates her," Marsha declared grimly.

"He doesn't. I'm just sure he doesn't." Annette began rummaging through the top drawer of her dresser. "Where's my cap?"

"Here." Marsha picked up the white cap that was lying on the bed beside her.

"To tell you the truth—" Annette walked over to the bed and took the cap, reaching for the beach bag at Marsha's feet "—I was half afraid that Kathleen wouldn't come back Sunday night. I thought dad might have fired her before he found someone to replace her."

"That's where he is now, isn't he, interviewing people?"

"I imagine so," Annette sighed, and stuffed her cap in the beach bag. "I know he was interviewing someone on Friday. I heard him on the telephone. If only I could think of something—some way to get them together."

"Maybe it's time we told daddy the truth," Marsha suggested, having never been very much in favor of the deception from the beginning.

Annette shook her head. "He'd just be as mad at us as he is at Kathleen. No, it will definitely have to be something else besides that. Come on, we'd better go downstairs. Kathleen's waiting for us."

THE ISOLATED STRETCH OF BEACH on Delaware Bay was deserted except for Kathleen and the two girls. Its location, a little over a mile from the house, made it one of their favorite haunts. The three of them often rode here on their ten-speed bicycles to spend an hour or an afternoon or a day.

Today, more than ever before, Kathleen welcomed the chance to get away from the house. Even though Jordan was gone, his ghost dominated the rooms, filling her with the sensation of his presence. In the privacy of her heart, she could admit that she had fallen in love with him, even if she would never say the words out loud.

Her gaze searched the beach for the girls. Marsha was wandering along the tideline, looking for whatever dubious treasure the waves might have washed ashore. Annette was floating on her air mattress, drifting closer to the beach.

Satisfied that they were safe, Kathleen lay back on her beach towel to bask in the warmth of the sun. Its glare was brilliant, reflected and intensified by the golden sand around her. Shielding her closed eyes with her forearm, Kathleen wished for the sunglasses in her beach bag, but she felt too enervated to move.

The strain of maintaining the professional mask of calm unconcern in front of the girls and Jordan, and, over the weekend, for Barry's benefit, had begun to take its toll. Nervous energy had drained her reserve strength to the point of near depletion.

A shadow fell across her. There was a gently indulgent curve to her mouth as she smiled and asked, "What did you find, Marsha?" She lifted her forearm away from her eyes, opening them slowly.

Her gaze didn't encounter Marsha's eager face. Instead it focused on muscular thighs, tanned a toasty brown with a liberal growth of dark hairs. Black swimming trunks covered slim hips, then revealed more hard golden-brown flesh tapering out to broad shoulders.

Aggressive lines carved out the face. A jutting chin with a cleft in its center formed the point of the strong jaw. Lean cheeks rose to powerful cheekbones, and thick black hair was brushed carelessly across a wide forehead. A straight nose, slightly flared, focused attention on black, spiked lashes outlining charcoal-gray eyes. Their gaze had just completed an equally thorough study of Kathleen and her bare flesh exposed by the two-piece bathing suit of copper gold.

"I—" Jordan placed emphasis on the pronoun "—found the note you left at the house."

Her stomach was somersaulting with sickening results while her heart raced at an alarming rate, making her feel weak and giddy. The torment of seeing him again so unexpectedly throbbed achingly in her throat.

All she could squeeze out was a tiny "Oh," and she propped herself up in a reclining position on one elbow.

"Dad!" came Annette's squeal of delight, followed by two sets of racing footsteps in the sand as she and Marsha ran toward him. "How long have you been here?"

"About a minute," he answered when they stopped breathlessly at his side. "Is this a private party, or am I allowed to join?"

"Of course you are," Marsha insisted.

Annette grabbed hold of his hand. "I've learned to do the butterfly. Come on, I'll show you!" She had barely started to lead him toward the water when she stopped, glancing at Kathleen. "Aren't you coming in, too?"

"Not right now." A tense smile accompanied her refusal.

It was useless to pretend she could lie back and forget he was there. Jordan's tall figure was like a magnet, drawing her gaze with an irresistible force. She watched him with his two daughters, listening to their laughter and happy voices, wishing hopelessly that she could be a part of that particular family unit.

Tears scalded her eyes. It all seemed so unfair. She had gone through the various stages of infatuation with other men, genuinely liking some and almost loving others, and kept waiting for the real thing to come along—the right man to enter her life. At twenty-five, she had found him—and knew not the joy but the agony of loving.

Her blurring vision saw Marsha wading ashore and Annette moving to follow. Kathleen lay back, covering her eyes with her hand and blinking rapidly to rid herself of the tears.

"WATER, WATER, EVERYWHERE, nor any drop to drink," Annette chanted as she caught the beach towel Marsha tossed her and began rubbing her wet skin. "I'm absolutely dying of thirst!" she declared with an exaggerated sigh. There was a decided gleam of intrigue in her gray eyes as she glanced at Kathleen lying silently in the sun. "Is it all right, Kathleen, if Marsha and I go back to the house for some cold drinks?"

Marsha opened her mouth to protest that she didn't want to go, but Annette immediately sent her a glowering look to shut up. Her lips closed together in a mutinous line.

"As long as you come straight back," was Kathleen's somewhat stiff reply.

"We will," Annette promised, tossing her towel over the beach bag and digging her fingers into her sister's resisting arm. "Come on, Marsha."

Marsha waited until they were out of Kathleen's hearing before she retorted angrily, "But I don't want to bike all the way back to the house and then all the way back here. If you're so thirsty, you can go by yourself."

"Being thirsty was just an excuse to leave so dad and Kathleen can be alone for a while," Annette patiently explained her strategy. "Honestly, Marsha, sometimes I wonder how you can possibly be my sister. You can be so dense at times."

"No, I'm not," Marsha retorted defensively. "I just think all these plans of yours are going to get us into a lot of trouble."

"You worry too much," Annette replied indifferently as she climbed onto her bike.

9

As the girls rode out of sight, Kathleen let her gaze slide to the bay. Jordan was wading ashore, bronze skin and dark hair gleaming wetly. Her heart constricted sharply and she knew her nerves would never tolerate a casual exchange of civility.

Rolling to her feet, she wandered idly toward the water, but in a direction that would not allow his path to intercept hers. Her destination was Annette's bright yellow air mattress, the waves licking its bottom at the water's edge. She pulled it farther onto the sand, then began wading into the water, intending to swim until the girls returned.

"Where are Annette and Marsha?" Jordan paused in ankle-deep water, several yards from Kathleen.

She stopped to answer, but turning only a fraction so that she wouldn't have to meet his gaze. "They rode to the house to bring back a cold drink."

"Where are you going?"

The water was almost to the calves of her legs. "For a swim."

She began wading farther out. The sloshing sound of her ungainly steps blocked her ears to the sound of Jordan's approach. Not until sunbrowned fingers closed over her forearm did she realize he had followed.

"The first rule of the water, Kathleen," he said as she pivoted around in alarm, "is never to swim alone. Let me take a breather and I'll join you."

Her widened gaze locked on the mouth that had formed her name. The sweet torment of his touch made her skin quiver in silent betrayal. She lifted her gaze to meet his, all the pent-up longing for his kiss revealed in the shimmering depths of her hazel eyes.

The sensually charged message was there for Jordan to read. His gray eyes darkened with a glittering fire, running over her curved figure, dwelling for tantalizing seconds on the shadowy cleft between her breasts, then blazing again on her face. His fingers tightened on her arm, almost imperceptibly pulling her toward him.

"Jordan, no," Kathleen whispered achingly, trying to deny how much she wanted his kiss.

"Yes." His other arm snaked around her bare waist, easily overcoming her token resistance. "Yes, dammit," he groaned when she shuddered against him.

His mouth opened over hers, warm and moist, devouring her lips with a hungry, demanding kiss. Kathleen felt herself drowning in a sea of heady sensations. Sliding her arms around the hard muscles of his shoulders, she surrendered to the man who already owned her heart and soul. It mattered little that he was intent on possessing her body as well. Glorying in the molding caress of his fingers on her back, she arched even closer to his male length, barely aware of the moment when he lowered her to the sand. His weight pressed her into the firm earth, gentle waves lapping and breaking over their legs and hips. They were both indifferent to all but the raging tide of their shared passion.

Instinctively, Kathleen's body moved sinuously beneath his in response to his hardness. Their driving need for gratification was bringing them both to the point of no return. Then, in a fleeting moment of sanity, Jordan broke free, rolling to his feet and drawing her with him.

His breathing was labored, his heart beating as rapidly as her own when he gathered her into his arms, holding her trembling body close to his own. Kisses were rained on her neck and throat.

"Jordan," Kathleen murmured, letting him know her need had not diminished.

"The girls will be back soon," he reminded her thickly, tangling his fingers in the damp tendrils of her fiery auburn hair and tipping her head back so he could gaze at her face. "I want to spend the afternoon making love to you, not a stolen moment."

Exquisite pain drew her breath in sharply. Quickly she buried her face in the tanned column of his neck, certain she would never again know the seating joy she felt at this moment. She couldn't speak, afraid that if she tried she would cry from sheer happiness.

"I'll find some excuse to drive them into Helen's to spend the night." Jordan spoke huskily against her hair. "We can either come back to the house or go to your apartment in town."

"I don't have one," she answered with a sobbing laugh. "I sublet my old one and hadn't found another that I could afford."

Now she wouldn't even need to look. Jordan wanted her.

His arms tightened almost cruelly around her. "You won't need to worry about that any more," he assured her firmly. "I'll take care of it. I've hired a woman to look after the girls. She starts on Wednesday. And on Thursday—" he smiled against her hair "—you and I will start looking for an apartment for you without any worries about whether *you* can afford it."

A cold knife was plunged into her heart, then twisted until the freezing pain was unendurable. Of all the romantic fools, Kathleen thought, she had to top the list! In her crazy, old-fashioned thinking, she had believed he would want to marry her. Instead, he was setting her up as his mistress.

Slowly her frozen arms unlocked and slid from around his shoulders. When her hands pressed against his naked chest in a mute request to be released, Jordan let her step away, smiling at her in that disturbing way that made her heart skyrocket even as it shattered.

Her eyes searched the beloved features of his ruggedly handsome face. Could she be satisfied with a tenuous existence as his mistress? Available whenever it suited him to see her? Willing to accept the crumbs of his attention left over after his work and his daughters? Never sharing the pain, the job, the monotony of everyday life?

"No." The negative word was issued as an answer to the assault of questions.

"What?" Jordan frowned, his gaze narrowing on her wan expression.

Kathleen glanced at him, startled to discover she had spoken aloud. The sight of him didn't lessen the truth of her answer. If she couldn't have all of him, then the heartbreak of having nothing couldn't be worse than the pain of only having a tiny piece.

"I said the answer was no," she repeated, turning away to walk toward her beach towel.

"No?" he repeated in disbelief, anger vibrating on the edge of his low voice. "No to what?"

She picked up the towel with a nonchalance that surprised her and began wiping away the grains of sand clinging to her skin. "No, I don't want you to make love to me."

Towering beside her, he ripped the towel from her grasp. "A minute ago you were damned eager!" he reminded her savagely.

Summoning all the courage of her convictions, Kathleen met the piercing steel of his gaze. "That was a minute ago."

89

"What kind of a woman are you?" his harsh voice taunted. "How can you turn passion on and off like a tap?"

There was a momentary impulse to tell him that passion could be turned off even if love couldn't, but she remained silent, holding out her hand for the towel. With a vicious flick of his wrist, he tossed it at her, long strides carrying him away from her to the spot where his own towel lay.

ANNETTE BRAKED HER BIKE to a halt short of the stretch of sandy beach. Her gaze centered on the two figures beyond, separated by several yards of golden sand.

She tossed a disgruntled look at Marsha. "Would you look at that?" she grumbled. "I'll bet they haven't said one word to each other since we left. This is beginning to get exasperating!"

WITH THE RETURN of the two girls, Jordan sot off for the house, stating that he had paperwork to do. But his gaze had flicked sardonically to Kathleen, and she had known she was responsible for the suppressed violence in his stride.

He didn't know or care how difficult the decision had been. It was just as well, Kathleen decided. It was better that he didn't realize she loved him, or at least that she loved him with such a deep and abiding emotion.

Dinner that evening was an uncomfortable meal. Jordan's brooding silence dominated the table as he barely touched the food. For once, not even Annette was her usual talkative self, a victim, too, of the tense undercurrents in the air. Kathleen had forced herself to eat, although the food was utterly tasteless.

When the dessert had been served and Kathleen had eaten as much as her constricting throat would swallow, Annette rose from the table.

"Marsha and I will wash up, Kathleen," she announced, and began gathering the dessert plates. "You can go into the living room and relax with dad."

"No, I'll help," Kathleen inserted quickly. She didn't trust herself to be alone with Jordan, not even for a few minutes.

"Neither Marsha nor I helped with dinner, so we'll clean up," Annette insisted.

"That doesn't matter. I—"

"Let them do it," Jordan interrupted curtly. "I want to speak to you, Kathleen."

Apprehension darkened her eyes as she met the pinning thrust of his. It was all she could do to remain in her chair and not race from the room.

"There, you see!" Annette declared brightly. "It's a direct order from your boss, Kathleen. You have to obey."

It wasn't his words that made her obey, it was the ruthless line of his mouth. Not for an instant did Kathleen doubt that Jordan would forcibly drag her into the living room if she attempted to refuse.

"Very well," she submitted, trying not to sound as trapped as she felt.

Awkwardly she rose from the table, her screaming nerves aware of Jordan following her as she walked into the living room. Blood was hammering through her veins, increasing the throbbing pain in her temples. Her legs were quickly turning to rubber, but they succeeded in carrying her to an armchair.

Jordan didn't sit down. He stood beside her chair, his hands thrust deeply into his pockets. Bending her head slightly down, Kathleen stared at the nervous twisting of her clasped hands, aware of his eyes upon her and unable to meet them.

"What did you want to talk to me about?" she asked tightly.

There was a movement beside her, then his hand touched the auburn fire of her hair. Kathleen barely stopped herself in time from jerking her head away from his touch.

"You didn't really want me to accept your word as final this afternoon, did you?" The statement was issued roughly, faintly accusing and faintly angry that she should play games with him.

The touch of his fingers was unendurable. It intensified the desire to know again the rapture of his caress. Kathleen didn't care what interpretation Jordan placed on her actions as she rose from the chair and took a hurried step away from him.

Had she wanted him to accept her answer? Probably not, she thought, but not for the reason Jordan assumed. With her, it was not simply lust.

"Yes, I did," she replied shortly.

The thick carpet muffled the sound of his footsteps. His hands lightly gripped the soft flesh of her upper arms, drawing her shoulders back against his chest. Her breath was stolen by his firm touch. Fire raced through her veins, melting her bones so that she was incapable of movement.

"I want you, Kathleen," he declared with husky forcefulness.

She was nearly caught in the undertow of her own desire for him.

"I know you want me," she agreed, "as your mistress, your lover." She swallowed, trying to ease the choking tightness of her throat. "You're something of a hypocrite, Jordan. You don't want me to live in the same house with you for fear of what your daughters and others might think, but you're willing to set me up in an apartment so you can see me whenever you feel the urge."

Jordan stiffened, his fingers momentarily biting into her flesh, then he released her entirely and walked away. Her knees trembled, threatening to give way, but she managed to stand erectly.

His back was turned to her. "What did you want?" His voice vibrated harshly over her.

"Something with more of a future," Kathleen admitted. "Some day I want a home and children. I want to become involved in my husband's life and have him become equally involved with mine."

"You could still have that. Later," he replied curtly.

"Not if I became emotionally involved with you," she answered, as if she wasn't already.

There was an abrupt movement of his head to the side. In a gesture of weariness, his hand rubbed the back of his neck, rumpling the silken ebony of his hair.

"My marriage to Rosalind, the girls' mother, showed me that marriage was not for me," he said tautly. "We loved each other—I didn't mean to imply that we didn't—but the bond of that love had begun to disintegrate when she died. You see, she didn't like my job, the travel and the many days away from home that it demanded. She had a congenital heart defect. It didn't prevent her from leading a normal life, but when she contracted a virulent form of influenza, it was ultimately the cause of her death. Quite rightly she wanted me to spend more time with her and our family, and it had become a source of conflict between us. A woman deserves her husband's time and attention, and I can't afford that. I never again want to hear meaningless apologies that I know will be repeated after the next bitter argument. I've had my share of tearful goodbyes and bittersweet reunions."

Kathleen brushed a hand across her face. The sting of tears was in her eyes. "Then let's not prolong our goodbye, Jordan," she said in a choked voice. "I can't offer you a casual affair, and you can't give me what I want. If we make the break now, there won't be any opportunity for recriminations by either of us."

"That's true." He took a deep breath but didn't turn around.

Proudly Kathleen lifted her chin, needing the gesture for her own benefit. "I'll leave in the morning. You said you'd hired a replacement. There's no need for me to stay until Wednesday. It may take her a few days to get used to where everything is, but I'm sure she'll manage."

"I'll tell the girls," Jordan stated flatly.

She had to press her lips tightly together to check the involuntary sob of pain. "I'll...I'll go and start packing."

Walking shakily, she started from the living room. By the time she reached the hall, she was practically running.

The tears refused to be held back and streamed down her cheeks.

MARSHA WAS SLUMPED morosely in the kitchen chair. Annette was standing behind another, her knuckles whitely gripping its back. Her resentful gray eyes were watching the violent swinging of the kitchen door, its action the result of her father's suppressed anger when he had left the room seconds before.

"I told you none of this would work," mumbled Marsha, tears hovering at the corners of her blue eyes.

"What I don't need from you is a bunch of I-told-you-sos!" Annette snapped.

Marsha's chin trembled. "Don't you start yelling at me. This was all your idea," she retorted in a quivering voice. "And now Kathleen's leaving."

Silently Annette acknowledged that she was unfairly releasing her frustrations on her sister. None of her protests, pleas or accusations that her father was breaking his word had made the least impression on him. She had not been able to persuade him that Kathleen should stay even a day longer, much less permanently.

"She isn't leaving for good," Annette stated with a determined set of her jaw, the telltale gleam of battle in her eyes.

Marsha simply looked at her and said nothing. She had witnessed the bitter argument between her older sister and her father and shuddered at the thought that there might be another.

It was useless to appeal to Annette that she should be sensible. It would only start an argument between them, and she already felt miserable enough knowing that Kathleen was leaving in the morning. Marsha couldn't summon much hope that any plan Annette might come up with would be any more successful than her others.

SAYING GOODBYE TO ANNETTE and Marsha and knowing she must never see them again had been the second hardest thing Kathleen had ever done. The hardest had been walking away from Jordan.

For the lack of any other place to stay, Kathleen had moved in with Maggie and Betty. She had gone through the motions of resuming the threads of her life, reapplying at the employment agency and going out on job interviews, but she was a brittle shell of her former self. She existed in a vacuum of intense heartache.

In the three weeks since she had left Jordan's home, the impossible had happened, instead of gradually forgetting him, she was thinking of him more and more each day. The decision she had made was lived over and over again. Sometimes she was positive she had been right to leave and other times she was certain she had been a fool not to snatch at a few fleeting moments of sublime happiness in his embrace. Wrapping her arms around her waist, she tried to fight off the shiver of excruciating pain and huddled into a tighter ball in the armchair. Her watch indicated that it was time to get ready for another job interview, but she didn't move, not even when the telephone rang.

93

She listened to its shrill demand, waiting for it to fall silent. It was probably Maggie or Barry. They phoned often whenever she was alone during the day. Wryly her mouth twisted, guessing that they feared she would attempt suicide. She hadn't quite sunk to that depth of depression yet and doubted that she would, no matter how unbearable the pain became.

The telephone stopped ringing, then started again. Sighing, Kathleen uncurled from the chair and walked to answer it. Tucking her hair behind her ear, she lifted the receiver.

"Hello," she said indifferently.

There was a crackle of interference, then an achingly familiar voice answered, "Kathleen?"

Her fingers clutched the receiver in a death grip. A giddiness buckled her knees as she sank onto the straight-backed chair beside the phone.

"Jordan?" she whispered after a panicked silence when she was certain she had imagined his voice on the other end.

"Yes." It was his voice, tense and strained, but it was his voice.

"How—why—" Tears spilled from her eyes. She should hang up the telephone, but she couldn't.

"I had to phone you. The employment agency gave me your number," he explained tautly.

There was more interference and Kathleen asked, "Where are you?"

"In Arabia."

"But—" She glanced at her watch. "The time—"

"Yes," Jordan interrupted, "I know, but I couldn't sleep. I've been thinking about you—which shows you the state of my mind if I have to phone you at three o'clock in the morning here. Kathleen, I—"

The connection was broken up. "I didn't hear you. What did you say?" she asked frantically.

"Damn!" The muttered curse followed her question. "Kathleen, I'll be flying back this Friday. I have to see you."

"Jordan, no," Kathleen protested, her heart breaking all over again as she spoke. "There's no point."

"I can't leave things the way they are."

"I can't go through this again, please," she begged. "I haven't changed my mind."

"We can't talk on the phone. I—"

Kathleen didn't dare see him again. She ached so much for the sight of him she knew she would give in to whatever he asked. She loved him too much. Even his voice was making her regret the adamancy of her statement.

Before she let him persuade her to reconsider, she very slowly replaced the telephone receiver on its cradle. She stared at it, its blackness blurring into the ebony color of his hair.

It started ringing again as she guessed that it would.

She rose from the chair and walked slowly into the small kitchen, turning on the radio as loud as it would go.

"KEEP MRS. PRENTISS in the kitchen until I come in there," Annette ordered.

"What are you going to do?" Marsha looked at her with dubious curiosity.

"I'm going to send a telegram to Mrs. Prentiss telling her that she's fired as of today," Annette announced, opening the study door.

"You can't do that!" her sister cried in astonishment. "She won't leave on your say-so."

"It won't be mine." Annette tossed her head in an airy manner. "It will be dad's."

"You can't do that!" Marsha repeated her previous exclamation. "He'll be home in three days! He'll be furious when he finds out—and you can bet he *will* find out! There isn't any way you can pretend that he sent the telegram, because he's going to know he didn't!"

"Of course he's going to know, but let's hope if the rest of my plan works, he isn't going to care."

"The rest of your plan? Annette," Marsha began hesitantly, "what's the rest of your plan?"

"You'd better get out to the kitchen and keep Mrs. Prentiss occupied," Annette reminded her.

"I'm not going anywhere until I find out what you're doing," her sister refused.

Annette's mouth thinned into a grim line.

"Oh, all right. I'm going to call Kathleen after Mrs. Prentiss leaves, and I'll ask her to come stay with us."

"She won't come," Marsha sighed.

"Yes, she will, *if*—" there was extra emphasis put on the qualifying word "—she believes that Mrs. Prentiss left of her own accord and you and I are here all alone."

"Kathleen will simply tell us to go and stay with Aunt Helen."

"If she does, I'll tell her that Aunt Helen is sick. She'll believe me. And she'll come out here, too. I know she cares about us, and she would never let us stay alone in the house."

"But what about when dad comes home on Friday? What are you going to do then?"

Annette's eyes rounded with false innocence. "He'll find Kathleen here, won't he? I've told you what I'm going to do, now you'd better go out to the kitchen and keep Mrs. Prentiss busy."

95

10

"How did the job interview go today?" Maggie slid a searching look across the small table to Kathleen.

Her face was nearly colorless, a faint blue shadow beneath eyes that were rimmed with red and partially swollen. Kathleen didn't meet her friend's gaze as she pushed the macaroni and cheese around on her plate.

"I forgot about it," she shrugged the indifferent answer. Jordan's phone call had blocked out every thing in her mind but him.

Maggie darted a knowing glance at Betty and silently shook her head. Profound concern was visible in both their expressions. The dispirited, sad girl at the table with them bore only a surface resemblance to the calm and competent nurse with an ever-ready smile that they had always known.

The telephone rang and Kathleen nearly jumped out of her chair. Brilliant green flecks of apprehension replaced the troubled dullness of her eyes. Maggie and Betty exchanged another look.

"I'll answer it," said Maggie, and rose from the table.

Paralyzed, her pulse fluctuating madly, Kathleen watched Maggie walk to the telephone and lift the receiver. Unconsciously she was holding her breath, afraid that it was Jordan and afraid that it was not.

"It's for you, Kathleen." Maggie held out the telephone to her.

"Who is it?" She released the breath she had been holding with a rush.

"A young girl," was the curious reply.

A shudder of disappointment raced through her. It was insane. She would have refused to talk to Jordan if he had called, so why did the news that it wasn't him hurt so much? Kathleen forced herself to walk to the telephone, speaking into it dully.

"Kathleen?" a frantically eager voice asked. "This is Annette."

Kathleen tensed, her nerves drawn taut. "Yes, Annette?" she replied in a brittle tone.

"I'm sorry to be calling you, but I didn't know what else to do." Something resembling a sob of panic punctuated the explanation.

Her hand tightened its grip on the receiver until her knuckles were white. "What's wrong? Your father? Has something happened to him? Is he hurt? Was there an accident?" Her fear-ridden questions tumbled after each other, not allowing Annette time to answer any of them.

"No, no, he's all right. At least, I think he is," was the qualifying answer. "Oh, Kathleen, it's Mrs. Prentiss, the lady that father hired when you left. She's walked out. She's left! Marsha and I are here all alone, and I don't know what to do! I've tried to reach dad, but I can't get through, and Aunt Helen is sick so she can't come. I didn't know who else to call. Marsha is terrified. Kathleen, can you come? Here? Tonight?"

"She just walked out without giving notice? Without making sure there was someone to stay with you girls?" Kathleen repeated in angry disbelief.

"Yes," Annette gulped. "She said we could fend for ourselves." A pause. "If you can't come, Kathleen, I don't know what we're going to do!"

"I'll be there within an hour," she promised.

"Will you stay?"

"Until your father comes home on Friday," Kathleen answered, suddenly feeling trapped. But there wasn't anything else she could do. She couldn't leave the girls alone in that big country house, and she certainly couldn't bring them here to Maggie's apartment. There wasn't room.

After she had hung up the receiver, she explained to Maggie and Betty the situation at the Long home with an economy of words. She could see by their expressions that they thought she was wrong to involve herself with the family again, but they didn't say a word. Kathleen sent up a silent prayer of gratitude for being blessed with understanding friends.

"DID YOU SEE HOW HAPPY Kathleen was to see us again?" Marsha sighed contentedly, her eyes bright and vivid blue. "She was practically crying."

"So were you," Annette returned, changing records on the stereo.

"I didn't realize how much I missed her." Self-consciously Marsha studied her fingers twisting in her lap. "It's going to be awful when she leaves again."

"Oh, ye of little faith." The blond cap of hair bobbed back and forth in a hopeless gesture, "It's very possible that she won't leave again, you know."

"You're forgetting that dad comes home tomorrow," Marsha reminded her.

"No, I'm not forgetting that. I'm counting on it." Then thoughtfully, "I wonder how Kathleen knew dad was coming home on Friday?"

EVERY SOUND HAD KATHLEEN TENSING. She was living on the raw edge of her nerves and had been since she had awakened that morning. It was Friday, and Jordan was due home.

For two days she had ignored the sword suspended above her head, stretching each moment in his house with his daughters to the fullest possible enjoyment. Now the sword would fall, and heaven only knew the damage it might do.

Kathleen looked at the kitchen clock again—she didn't know why. She had no idea what time he would come. Logic said it would be late in the afternoon, and it was barely eleven o'clock now.

Her hand trembled as it spread the chocolate frosting over the yellow cake. The sound of a car motor went through her like an electric shock, immobilizing her. It stopped, then a car door slammed. The knife was dropped onto the counter top as Kathleen's hand flew to her hair, a feminine gesture of insecurity.

With her stomach doing somersaults, she turned toward the door, trying not to devour Jordan with her eyes when he walked in. There was a haggard pallor to his face, aquiline features strained to the point of tautness, gray eyes clouded with inner turbulence.

His hand raised, passing in front of his eyes, then he stared at her again. "I saw your car." His expression hardened. "What are you doing here, Kathleen?" he demanded with a tinge of bitterness. She blanched and turned away, but instantly long strides carried him to her side. "I don't care why you're here," he muttered, his fingers closing over her shoulders. "It's just hell I've been through—wanting you—needing you, and you wouldn't even answer the damned phone!" he cursed hoarsely.

"Jordan." His touch was turning her bones to molten lava. She wanted to mm into his arms and invite his caress, but she forced herself to remain rigidly unresponsive. "I'm here because of the girls. They weren't able to reach you, although they tried several times. The woman you hired walked out and left them. Helen is sick, so they called me. I told them I would stay until you came back."

The cruel pressure of his fingers forced her around. "What did you say?"

"I said I'm leaving." The words ripped at her heart like a sword. "I'll be gone within the hour."

"No!" Jordan snapped.

"Yes, I—" Kathleen stared at the loosened tie around his neck, unable to look into the face she loved so desperately.

"No, I mean about Mrs. Prentiss!"

Startled, she lifted her head, gazing into the piercing gray eyes shadowed by the thick gathering of his brows in frowning demand.

"She walked out. She just quit and left the girls without anyone to stay with them," Kathleen explained again.

"The hell she did!" Abruptly he released her and walked with impatient, springing strides to the swinging door leading to the dining room. "Annette! Marsha!" he barked.

They walked through the door a split second after he had called them. Stunned, Kathleen watched in confusion, rooted to the floor where Jordan had left her.

"Hi, dad!" Annette greeted him with her usual bright smile. "You're home earlier than we thought."

Marsha's smile was much. more hesitant, intimidated by the glowering look on his face. "Hi, dad."

"Kathleen was just telling me that Mrs. Prentiss isn't here." His expression was grimly forbidding.

Annette licked her lips. "That's right. She just walked out on us, said she was fed up with taking care of a house and Marsha and me. You don't know what a panic we were in until we finally reached Kathleen," she declared with an exaggerated sigh.

"She quit, is that right?" Jordan repeated.

"Yes, just like that!" Annette snapped her fingers to indicate the abruptness of Mrs. Prentiss' departure.

"Then would you mind explaining to me why she left a message at the company's main office, saying that since I had *fired* her, she was entitled to two weeks' severance pay and demanded that she receive it?" His dark head was tipped to the side, accusing gray eyes fixed on the girls.

Annette returned the look blankly while Marsha shifted uncomfortably from one foot to the other. "I don't know what you're talking about, dad," Annette laughed shortly. "She quit."

"What about the telegram *I* supposedly sent her?" Jordan queried, an arrogant arch to one dark brow. "Would you know anything about that?"

"A telegram?" Annette breathed, and glanced hesitantly at Marsha.

"We'd better tell him the truth," Marsha murmured her answer.

"Yes, I think you'd better," he agreed grimly.

"Well, you see, dad," Annette began, wandering almost absently toward the kitchen table, as if she wanted to put distance between herself and her father, "actually I'm the one who sent the telegram telling Mrs. Prentiss she was fired. We—Marsha and I—wanted Kathleeen back. And that seemed one sure way to do it."

"It didn't occur to you that Kathleen might not want to come back, did it?" Jordan accused.

"No," Annette replied decisively.

"Annette—" Marsha glanced at her sister "—we'd better tell him the rest."

"The rest of what?" he demanded, eyeing both girls in an ominous way.

Kathleen's curiosity was thoroughly aroused, especially because Marsha looked so terribly guilty. Annette, as always, seemed to be more sure of her position.

"Well, dad, there are a few things you don't know," Annette admitted, then paused.

"Such as?" he prompted.

"Such as how Kathleen came to work for us in the first place," Marsha inserted in a small voice.

"Oh?"

There was a wealth of meaning in that one word, and his younger daughter quailed at the sound.

Kathleen assumed they were referring to the interview, although at this point she didn't see what relevance it had.

"Remember the mistake on her application?" Annette spoke up. "Actually, Kathleen didn't make a mistake. We, mainly me, forged another application, changing her age, so you would think she was older."

"And Aunt Helen really didn't recommend her," Marsha added. "We changed her letter, too."

"No!" Kathleen breathed, unable to believe that any of this could be true.

"I'm sorry, Kathleen," Marsha apologized. "I know how angry dad was when he found out, but it was the only way we could think of for you to get the job."

"But why?" Kathleen frowned, moving to stand beside Jordan as he faced the two girls.

"Because—" Annette studied her father for a long, considering second "—we thought it was time daddy got married again. We liked you the minute we met you and hoped that daddy would, too."

"So you took it upon yourselves to find me a wife!" he accused harshly.

"You didn't seem to be able to find anyone halfway decent. We didn't think we would do any worse than you," Annette shrugged. "It seems—" an impish light entered her gray eyes "—that we didn't do too bad a job either. I mean, you fell in love with her and she fell in love with you. And that was the whole point of our plan."

"It was, was it?" Jordan released a slow, angry breath.

"And," Annette said, considering thoughtfully her father's hooded look, "if I have timed this confession correctly, about now Marsha and I should leave the room so you and Kathleen can get things straightened out between you. You don't have to be angry at her anymore, dad. We're the ones who deceived you, not Kathleen."

The air was charged with unspoken words. Covertly Kathleen glanced at Jordan, unable to decipher the enigmatic light in his gray eyes. Without a word, Annette moved away from the table with Marsha following more hesitantly. The silence crackled with electricity, when they were gone.

"Do you love me?" Jordan asked at last, an arrogant mask over his ruggedly handsome features.

Kathleen turned her head away. "Yes," she answered calmly, her heart beating so fast that she was certain he could hear it. "But it doesn't change anything. I want to share more than just the physical side of love with you." His hand touched her cheek and she jerked away. "Please, I don't have much strength where you're concerned. Don't tempt me. I know now how much you want me, and I want you, too, but—"

"Want you!" The harshly spoken exclamation indicated that Kathleen had understated his need.

Her movement away from him was roughly checked. His hand captured her face, lifting it to meet his descending mouth. Her resistance lasted only for an instant as his hard, demanding kiss aroused the response she had known it would.

Circling her arms around his waist, she allowed herself to be swept into the whirlpool. His hands slid down, molding her pliant flesh against the hard contours of his male body. His mouth parted her willing lips, sending brilliant quicksilver fires of ecstasy through her veins.

When mere kisses could no longer satisfy their elemental desire, Jordan drew his head away, burying his mouth along the side of her hair. The drum beat of his heart was beneath her head. He shuddered against her as he fought for control, "Now do you understand?" he muttered hoarsely. "I don't simply want you. I need you, Kathleen, I haven't been worth a damn since you left. I made such a mess of things in Arabia that the company had to send over another man to straighten it out."

"Jordan darling," Kathleen whispered achingly, winding her arms more tightly around him.

"I couldn't open my eyes without picturing you nor breathe without catching a hint of your fragrance. I kept remembering the feel of your body in my

arms and the taste of your lips. It was your voice I heard on everyone's lips."
He held her more fiercely and shuddered again. "They all thought I was mad,
and I am. No woman has ever destroyed me the way you have. I love you,
Kathleen, and I can't live without you. I haven't even the strength to try."

"Neither have I," she sighed, lifting her head for him to see the shimmering
glow of rapture in her eyes. "I love you, Jordan—I could say it a thousand times."

He smiled, deepening the cleft in his chin. "Maybe after a million times I
might have heard it enough. Marry me, Kathleen. Nothing else will satisfy
either of us."

A diamond tear slipped from the corner of her eye. "Yes."

Jordan kissed away the tear. Unable to stop, he went on kissing her, lingering on each feature until he finally reached her trembling lips. Then,
shaken again by her scorching response, he held her away from him, his gray
eyes drinking in her radiance.

"I should be furious with Annette and Marsha," he said in a husky voice
that sent shivers down her spine. "But how can I be angry with them for trick-
ing you into being here waiting for me when I came home? I thought I was
going to have to batter down doors to get to see you."

Kathleen wanted to go back into his arms, but she let him keep her at
arm's length. "I can't believe they went to such lengths to have me hired,"
she murmured.

"I have a hunch—" his mouth quirked with dry amusement "—that they
arranged a few other things to keep you here so I would fall in love with you.
I don't regret it. I'm just glad they love you as much as I do."

"I love them, too," Kathleen smiled. Even if she hadn't already loved them
before, she certainly would have now, since they had brought her to the man
she loved.

"Some day we'll find out the whole story and the way you and I were
maneuvered by a pair of adolescents. Right now—" the smile was crinkling his
eyes, the rich gray color of velvet "—I suppose we should let them know how
successful they've been. That is, if they haven't been listening at the door." His
gaze swung to the dining-room door. "Have you been listening, Annette?"

There was a moment of silence, then the door was pushed open. Annette
sauntered into the room, followed by Marsha, who shyly smiled at Kathleen.
There was a complacent gleam in Annette's gray eyes as she looked at the two
of them.

"Congratulations," Annette offered, trying not to grin too widely. "When's
the wedding?"

"As soon as it can be arranged," Jordan answered.

"Can we be in it?" Marsha asked.

"Who else would I ask?" Kathleen laughed.

"Tomorrow we'll have to go and buy your wedding dress," Annette declared, "and gowns for Marsha and me. Then we—"

"Hold it!" Jordan interrupted. "There'll be no more planning by you girls. You've done all you're going to do—and don't think that there won't be some punishment meted out before this is over. Whatever future plans that you have forming in your minds, you can forget."

"Actually—" an impish light glittered in Annette's eyes "—I was thinking that it might be nice to have a baby brother."

"I'll handle any future additions to this family," he stated firmly, reaching for Kathleen's hand, "without any help from you or Marsha!"

A rush of delicious warmth surged through Kathleen's veins as Jordan drew her to his side, fitting her into the crook of his arm. Annette shrugged her shoulders, but the silver light didn't leave her eyes.

"If you say so, dad," she submitted. "We'll let you handle things from now on. Since you probably have plans to make, is it all right if we go and call Aunt Helen and tell her the news?"

"Go on," he agreed. When the dining-room door swung shut behind them he glanced at Kathleen, his attention centering on her dimpling smile. "What's that smile all about?" he asked, touching a fingertip to the closest dimple.

"I was just pitying the poor man that Annette sets her sights on when she's grown up. He won't stand a chance," she murmured, unconsciously moving her cheek against his hand in a caressing gesture.

"If she picks the right man, she'll be the one who won't stand a chance," Jordan corrected, turning her into his arms and studying her upturned face. "Now, about our son..."

About the Author

Janet Dailey, who passed away in 2013, was born Janet Haradon in 1944 in Storm Lake, Iowa. She attended secretarial school in Omaha, Nebraska, before meeting her husband, Bill. The two worked together in construction and land development until they "retired" to travel throughout the United States, inspiring Janet to write the Americana series of romances, setting a novel in every state of the Union. In 1974, Janet Dailey was the first American author to write for Harlequin. Her first novel was *No Quarter Asked*. She has gone on to write approximately ninety novels, twenty-one of which have appeared on the *New York Times* bestseller list. She won many awards and accolades for her work, appearing widely on radio and television. Today, there are over three hundred million Janet Dailey books in print in nineteen different languages, making her one of the most popular novelists in the world. For more information about Janet Dailey, visit www.janetdailey.com.

OPEN ROAD
INTEGRATED MEDIA

Open Road Integrated Media is a digital publisher and multimedia content company. Open Road creates connections between authors and their audiences by marketing its ebooks through a new proprietary online platform, which uses premium video content and social media.

CPSIA information can be obtained
at www.ICGtesting.com
Printed in the USA
JSHW031740200323
39185JS00001B/184